PERILS AND DANGERS

PERILS AND DANGERS

Peter Turnbull

This first world edition published in Great Britain 2001 by
SEVERN HOUSE PUBLISHERS LTD of
9–15 High Street, Sutton, Surrey SM1 1DF.
This first world edition published in the USA 2001 by
SEVERN HOUSE PUBLISHERS INC. of
595 Madison Avenue, New York, NY 10022.

British Library Cataloguing in Publication Data

Turnbull, Peter, 1950
    Perils and dangers
    1. Police – England – Yorkshire – Fiction
    2. Detective and mystery stories
    I. Title
    823.9'14 [F]

ISBN 0–7278–5672–3

Typeset by Palimpsest Book Production Limited,
Polmont, Stirlingshire, Scotland.
Printed and bound in Great Britain by
MPG Books Ltd, Bodmin, Cornwall.

One

In which a man is murdered.

S ophie Asquith disliked Nathan Ossler. She disliked him with an intensity which frightened her, an intensity which, she found, at times, bordered upon hatred. At times, she found, her feelings for him would cross even that dreadful boundary. His snarling at everything that moved, his shouting, his seething, evil temper, the way he used the vodaphone, gripping it until his knuckles whitened, baring his teeth and growling into it. It was the way he reduced the women around him to tears, the stream of secretaries, some lasting only a few hours before they voted with their feet, his long-suffering wife for whom it was less easy to vote with her feet. And the fact that Nathan Ossler was from the south of England didn't help endear him to Sophie Asquith who, being native to the Famous and Fayre City of York, disliked and distrusted anyone who came from south of the Humber, or west of the Pennines or north of the Tyne.

But it was a job, for Sophie Asquith it was a job. And she stuck at it because he paid cash, and she could go home each evening and because, unlike his wife or his present secretary, who had thus far remained in his employ longer than any previous secretary, Sophie Asquith saw little of

1

him. This suited her admirably, though it was still upsetting to see his secretary tapping away at her word-processor with him standing behind her shouting about this mistake or that, or seeing his wife curled up in floods of tears again, with him standing there shouting about the size of this bill or that frivolous purchase. Occasionally, he would bend down and push his face close up to hers just to make sure she clearly understood the reason for his displeasure. The present secretary, it seemed to Sophie Asquith, had the ability to switch herself off and let her employer's words and ill temper wash over her like a rock repeatedly submerged by heavy seas but always emerging again. His wife, it further seemed, had no such survivor skills to resort to. That Sophie Asquith was often privy to such displays of tyranny, she eventually realised, was the same reason why she never felt the edge of his tongue: she was the cleaning woman, the woman who "comes and does" and goes away again and, as such, in Ossler's eyes, just did not figure in the scheme of things. This, again, suited Sophie Asquith admirably. It made her job easier. But she felt for his secretary, and she felt more for his wife.

That particular Monday morning, Sophie Asquith had wheeled her elderly bottle-green cycle from the shed beside her small cottage to the road. The sun was well up, she would later recall, and the day already warm, requiring only a light skirt and blouse, though she had placed a cardigan in the pannier in case of a chill wind later in the day. It was June, and as always in the summer, the Vale of York baked under a relentless sun. The winters were bad, with nothing to stop the biting east wind keening across the flat landscape, and now, in the decline of her life, Sophie Asquith felt the winters more acutely, but she believed that to be able to live in the Vale when there wasn't an "R" in the month, made the winters bearable. That day was one such day which, she felt, made the last winter worth battling through and the memory of which, and of similar days, would keep her going through the winter to come. She sat on her bike, reversing herself ladylike into the saddle, though often she would envy the young, jean-clad female students who would mount cycles in the male way by swinging one of their legs over the frame, and she began the pleasant cycle ride from Towthorpe to Strensall which she completed in her usual thirty minutes. In Strensall, in a particular lane on the edge of the village, she dismounted in front of a house called "Thundercliffe Grange".

Thundercliffe Grange was a new build house, well set back from the road, mainly a bungalow but with a single second storey elevation being the master bedroom. The house was surrounded by neat, well-tended, if not manicured, gardens. She opened the wrought iron gate which squeaked and brought forth two barking Alsatians bounding across the lawn. The dogs ran aggressively towards Sophie Asquith until they were within twenty feet of her when their eyes focused, they recognised her and her scent and returned, at a trot, to the house.

Their tails were between their legs.

She thought it unusual. Usually, no, no, not usually, always, always, the two dogs bounded across the lawn, recognised her and then turned and returned to the house with their tails wagging. It seemed to Sophie Asquith that the dogs were worried about something.

Probably nothing.

Probably something.

She walked down the gravel-covered drive and turned

in front of the house and then down beside the left-hand side facing of the house, past the wheelie bins, hidden by a section of lattice fencing, and rested her cycle beside the side door. She opened the door. It was unlocked, but there was little unusual in that. Ossler, she had noticed, was an early riser and was often up and about by the time she arrived in the mornings, so much so that she was invited to enter the house should she find the side door unlocked. She stepped over the threshold and called "Hello . . . it's only me."

There was no reply. Her voice seemed to echo in the house and the dogs, she noticed, did not enter the house as they usually did when she opened the door, seeming as they did to enjoy the luxury of the open door rather than having to endure the indignity of the dog flap. That morning they remained outside, turning in tight circles, seemingly lost and confused. As if on automatic pilot, Sophie Asquith crossed the vestibule just inside the door and entered the kitchen and made herself a cup of tea. Mrs Ossler had invited her to "make herself at home in the kitchen", to help herself to tea or coffee and a sandwich if she felt hungry. No need to ask. And each morning she would arrive, leave her bike by the door and, whether or not anyone was in the kitchen, she would make herself a cup of tea. She couldn't function without it. It had become a necessity of life, a great aid to the emotional resilience she needed to help her get through another bruising day at the Ossler house and all its rantings and weeping. She settled in a chair at the kitchen table, puzzling over its formica top of yellow with a myriad of thin lines like a spiders web, which was not at all to her taste but, just as she had learned, was Nathan Ossler's taste. She sat back pulling her eyes away from the mesmeric attraction of the tabletop and puzzled again, this time at the silence of the house. It was not so much that such silence was unusual, no shouting, even first thing in the morning, no radio or early morning TV with the volume turned up too loud. Just silence.

Something's happened. Something *has* happened. The silence . . . the dogs . . .

The words came to Sophie Asquith's mind as a chill ran down her spine. The words came from nowhere, there was no trigger that she could identify or determine, no sight, no sound, perhaps just the absence of same, but if the trigger was anything, it was a mood, an ambience, an atmosphere. Her scalp began to crawl.

She stood slowly, nervously, with a growing fear, and began to walk about the house. Shortly after leaving the kitchen she saw the first dead person she had ever seen.

He was in the study, often referred to as the "workroom" at the rear of the house, with a window which looked out on to a wide lawn bounded by Leylandii shrubs. The room itself was small, made more so by the banks of filing cabinets, a desk with a word-processor atop and an armchair being the only soft furnishing in the room. He was slumped in the armchair. The upper front of his head was missing, as if blown off, and bits of scalp tissue and blood spots seemed to be splattered on the wall behind him. And there were the flies, by dint of the slightly open window, there were flies, scores of them, perhaps even in their hundreds. In fact, as she would often tell people whenever she related the tale in the months and years to come, it was the loud buzzing of same which, after checking the living-room, the dining-room, the television room and the downstairs bedroom, had finally obliged her to push open the study door to be met with a black, swirling swarm of the things. She had stepped back in an arm flailing frenzy, uttered a loud "ugh!" and then peered into the room and stared at Nathan Ossler, less the top of his head, and found herself remarking how still and quiet he could be with a little help.

She didn't scream. That was what came to surprise her the most as her mind would return to the event. She had always thought that she would scream should she ever chance upon a deceased person because, according to television and film, that's what women did. Her parents were deceased but they had died tragically in a fire and their bodies had been charred beyond recognition and so she had not seen them in death. She was now in her early middle years, lived quietly, all her relatives were alive and well, she had just not seen a dead body, and had always thought that when she did, that she would scream. But she didn't. Probably, she thought, probably it was because there was no sense of shock that someone would want to kill Nathan Ossler, that didn't surprise her at all. All she felt was a sense of relief, a sense of a weight being lifted from her that he was gone. Then she thought about the dogs and scurried to the vestibule, their food and water bowls were indeed empty. She filled the water bowl and the dogs, hearing the sound of running water, rushed into the house and each drank deeply. Sophie Asquith opened a can of dog food, gave them half each, sufficient to break their fast and which they ate ravenously. She replenished the water bowls and put them in the shed. She then ushered the dogs into the shed, and ensuring the window was open, shut the door behind her, leaving the dogs. Only then did she dial three nines.

It was the "just so" appearance of the house which surprised George Hennessey and also brought about his personal disapproval. It was, he thought, a "dead house". Even when all who dwelt within were alive and well physically, it was not emotionally, it would have been a "dead house", the-everything-in-its-place perfection, the sanitised atmosphere.

The house first. He viewed the house from the road, standing next to the constable in his white summer shirt, open-necked, who, in turn, stood next to one of the two gateposts across which a blue and white "police" tape had been strung. Police vehicles were parked on the road, including the black windowless mortuary van, ready to be reversed into the drive when the corpse was to be removed. It was not, Hennessey noted, an easy house to approach with felonious intent. The long drive was covered with gravel, no one could step on it without making a sound which, while not particularly loud in terms of volume, would carry a long distance, especially on a still summer's night. He had noticed this aspect of sound before, the way in which a loud "bang" will not arouse suspicion but a gentle, near imperceptible "click" would. In order to reach the house silently from the road, any person would have to leave the drive, step across a flower-bed and stand on the lawn and be thus quite exposed, standing or walking on an area of garden an infantryman would call "open ground". The front garden was lined with Leylandii shrubs, a plant Hennessey personally detested, and beyond that there was a wire fence about six feet high, neatly separating the garden from the neighbouring garden. Beyond the garden wall was a bed of roses, large and deep enough to prevent any felon from hopping over the wall and on to the lawn. No, it was not an easy building to approach without advertising your presence in some way. Hennessey ducked beneath the police tape and opened the gate which gave a loud "squeak" as he pushed it. Another deterrent to a silent approach to the house.

He walked a few feet down the drive, crunching the gravel as he did so and then stepped on to the lawn. On that June morning the house and garden presented a spectacle that he found pleasingly colourful. The green of the lawn and the Leylandii gave way to a long-fronted bungalow in the light coloured grey brick favoured in the Vale, beneath a red-tiled roof. Above all was an immense, almost cloudless blue sky.

Hennessey approached the house, stepped off the lawn on to the narrow stretch of gravel and instantly set two dogs barking from the direction of the left hand side of the house. It was, he noted, yet another deterrent to a silent, secret approach to the house. The front door of the house was open. He stepped across the threshold and it was then that he was met by the "just so" nature of the Ossler household. A Scenes of Crime Officer in white coveralls was photographing the house, every room from every aspect. A second and third Scenes of Crime Officer dusted for fingerprints. Sergeant Yellich stood in the hallway. He nodded and smiled at Hennessey.

"You look as though you are waiting for me, Yellich?"

"Heard you and saw you approaching, sir."

"And in doing so, just proved what I have been thinking. What have we got? A body, I believe?"

"Yes, boss. Back room downstairs. Messy, this one."

"Gunshot, you say?"

"Aye, boss. This is a solemn number and no mistake."

"Lead on, please."

Yellich walked along the corridor and stopped outside a door, deferentially stepping aside, opening the door for Hennessey, who entered the room.

The deceased lay slumped in an armchair in the cramped room. Flies still buzzed in large numbers. Louise D'Acre knelt on the floor. She stood as Yellich entered the room. She too was dressed in a white coverall. "Good morning, Chief Inspector."

"Dr D'Acre."

"A single victim, adult male. As you see, he appears to have died as a result of a gunshot wound to the head."

"Appears?"

"Yes, appears." Dr D'Acre held eye contact with Hennessey and then looked at the corpse. "You see the fact that the top of his head has been blown off doesn't mean to say that that was what killed him. At this stage, all I can say is that the gunshot wound, which is clearly evident, is contemporary with his death. It may very well be the cause of it, in fact it probably is. But only probably. He could have died just prior to being shot, he could even have died after being shot."

"After?"

"Oh yes, even a head wound of this nature is not necessarily fatal, at least not instantly so. You see, a cardiac arrest just prior or post to the gunshot wound is possible, as is death by poisoning just prior to the head injury. Mind you, within these four walls, I will say that were I a betting lady I would bet vast amounts of shekels that his death was caused by the gunshot. But forensic pathology is an exact science and betting doesn't enter into the assessment. Frankly, the attitude of slumping back in the chair is what suggests the gunshot to be the cause of death more than the wound itself. Strangely enough . . . you see he's not sitting in the chair, he's almost sliding out of it."

"Yes . . . ?"

9

"That suggests, but only suggests, that he was standing up when he was shot and the bullet sent him staggering backwards and he slumped into the chair. A cardiac arrest would have caused him to collapse forward, in which case he might expect to be found lying face down on the carpet, and poison . . . well depending on the type, it may have taken him in his sleep or in a sitting position. But strychnine, for example, would have induced convulsions in which the room would have been disturbed. Further, you see the fact that his body has remained in this position . . . no trail of blood for example . . . indicates instantaneous death from a single gunshot wound to the head."

"He had the top of his head blown off while he was standing up a little way in front of the armchair?"

"Well, yes . . . probably."

"That's good enough for me to be working on as a murder. No gun at the crime scene so there is not even an attempt to make it look like suicide."

"A suicide would have been more accurate."

"It seems accurate enough to me." Hennessey nodded at the body. "Didn't miss, did it? The bullet I mean."

"Well, the shot was accurate enough to be fatal, that I grant you, but if it was a suicide, you'd expect a more direct entry, here there is something a little 'chancy' about the angle of entry. It has the hallmarks of being a lucky shot or an accidental shot."

"Lucky?" Hennessey grinned. "That depends on your point of view." A flashbulb popped behind him.

"Indeed," Louise D'Acre smiled, sharing the joke. "But if the firearm was a handgun, it's difficult to see a rifle being used in a room as small as this, then the barrel, in the case of suicide, would be placed so." She pressed the tip of a slender

straightened finger at the centre of her forehead. "Or so . . ."
She placed the fingertip to the side of her head above her
ear. "Or so," placing her fingertip inside her mouth. "Or
even so," and placed her fingertip vertically under her chin.
"But here, as you see, the gun has entered the forehead at an
angle, as if the bullet travelled on a path which was parallel
to the nose, about forty-five degrees to the vertical, that sort
of angle."

"The gun was fired by a much shorter person?"

"Probably. Perhaps a taller person sitting down in the
chair in front of the word processor. But the point is that it's
not suicide, nor is it a calmly aimed bullet. And the muzzle of
the gun was at least two feet from the entry wound, there are
no carbon deposits or 'tattooing' which occur if the muzzle
of the gun was about two feet or less from the entry wound.
This is what we call a long-range wound which, despite its
name, means anything beyond two feet between muzzle and
wound."

"So, if he was standing in front of the chair, as if he got
up in response to someone coming into the room, possibly
unexpectedly, then the person holding the gun could have
been standing just inside the doorway?"

"Yes . . ." Louise D'Acre pursed her lips. "Yes, it's a
possibility."

"So we can safely rule out suicide?"

"You can't safely rule out anything at the moment. It's
far, far too early in the piece for any ruling out of anything.
But as always, I'll tell you all I can safely tell you once I
have completed the post-mortem."

"Time of death?"

"TOD?" Louise D'Acre pondered the corpse. "Open
window, hence the flies, no artificial cooling or heating of

11

the house . . . a little warmer in the house than out this time of year, rigor well established, as are the flies. Always a good indicator of TOD are our flying friends, annoying as you may find them Chief Inspector, they are the forensic pathologist's best friend and they have helped solve many a murder mystery: day clothing rather than dressing-gown. You and I could put our heads together on this one . . . it's ten a.m. now approximately, Monday, more than twenty-four hours ago – less than forty-eight hours ago . . . but that's tentative, Chief Inspector. I wouldn't allow myself to be held to it."

"Agreed."

"I understand your need for something to work on, Chief Inspector, but I can't commit myself to a narrower time window until after the p.m."

"Again, agreed and understood, but I can assume that he was alive at ten a.m. on Saturday last, and was deceased by ten a.m. yesterday. About?"

"About. Yes, you can assume that. Probably. Capital 'A' and 'P' respectively, and that's sticking my neck out much more than is professionally sensible. I'm doing it to throw a bone to a hungry dog, you understand."

"Woof!" Hennessey said softly, with a warm smile.

"Well, I've done all I can here. If you've got all the snapshots you want . . . ?"

"It's a shooting expression."

"What?"

"Snapshot. People who blow birds out of the sky with shotguns, a rapid shot at a sudden and unexpected target as opposed to a careful aim is known as a 'snapshot'. Photographers hijacked it from the shooting set." Louise D'Acre glanced sideways at Hennessey. "I'll die a wiser woman for that."

"But I think we've finished. They should be by now. I'll check with my sergeant." Hennessey left the room, sought the youthful Sergeant Yellich, returned to the room and advised Dr D'Acre that the police had no further reason to detain the body and that it may be removed to the York District Hospital.

Hennessey observed the corpse being placed in a body bag and carried to the mortuary van, which had by then been reversed down the drive to the house. He then walked to the side of the house to the shed in which two Alsatians, whimpering and barking in turn, were held, and then to the rear of the house, a second expanse of lawn, neatly cut, surrounded by flower-beds. Beyond the flower-beds a stand of Leylandii stood completely round the three sides of the rear garden, and beyond the Leylandii, more six-foot high fencing. All, he noted, was shipshape and Bristol fashion, as the expression had it. He returned to the house and found Yellich. "He knew his attacker."

"Yes, boss." Yellich nodded. "Solemn guy. The attacker I mean. Very solemn."

"Why do you say that?"

"Same thoughts as you I should think, boss. No sign of a break-in, no sign of disturbance, no sign of a robbery, jewellery still in the bedroom plus a fair bit of cash . . . the impression is that the murderer came here with murder on his mind, with murderous intent, and he didn't hang about. He got into the house, got past the dogs, did the deed and went away again. Probably all over in a minute or two. Very, very, very solemn. Very solemn indeed."

"Who found him?"

"The cleaning lady. Lady called . . ." Yellich consulted his notepad. "Asquith. Good political name that. Sophie

13

Asquith, fifty-three years old, lives in the next village, cleans for the Osslers each weekday morning. She called three nines . . . patrol bobby investigated, he called CID. I came, got SOCO here and Dr D'Acre, it being definitely suspicious."

"Oh, most definitely."

"Young woman came to the home while we were here, a woman called Tulse. Ruth Tulse. She has an address in York, Rawcliffe Lane, Clifton. She gets the bus out. She's employed as Mr Ossler's secretary, five days a week, nine to five with an hour for lunch."

"Ossler being the victim?"

"That's the presumption at this stage, sir. But, frankly, there's no one else it could be, so it's a safe bet that it is."

"We can't proceed on presumptions or safe bets."

"Of course, sir, but I saw no reason to detain either the secretary or the housekeeper. We have their addresses."

"Fair enough. What do we know about him? Mr? What did you say his name was?"

"Ossler."

"Ossler. What do you know about him?"

"Early days yet, boss. Haven't done our CR checks yet. The housekeeper says he's a sort of local Mr Ten Per Cent. No one business, but fingers in many pies which are as varied as they are many, by all accounts."

"Lived alone? There's no feel of a family about this house."

"Married. No children."

"Oh dear." Hennessey grimaced, distraught next of kin.

"The secretary told us where his wife would be found. She, the wife, visits her brother each weekend. She often stays over Sunday evening and returns on the Monday. We have the brother's address provided by the secretary. I have sent a car to bring her back . . . an address in Tang Hall."

"Tang Hall!" Hennessey raised his eyebrows. "Her brother lives in Tang Hall and she lives here?"

"Aye. Moved up, wouldn't you say, boss?"

"Moved well up I'd say. She certainly didn't marry down. Tang Hall to here is a leap in the right direction in any man's language. Right, can you go and see the lady who found him, and then visit the secretary, anything could be relevant at this stage, you know the drill."

"OK, boss."

"I'll hang around here and have a word with Mrs Ossler. You know the ID's going to be a problem, half his head blown away like that."

"I noticed a tattoo on his right forearm, boss, had it photographed. I saw his wallet on the dresser in the bedroom, had his driving licence in."

"That'll have his DOB."

"That's what I thought. Feed his name into Criminal Records, plus his numbers, might get a result. If we get a result, we'll have his fingerprints on record, if we can match them, we've got a positive ID."

"Can you do that before those two visits, please. It'll save said distressed relative from having to view her dear departed *sans* his head."

"Right, boss. Good as done."

Hennessey, lightweight summer jacket and trousers and topped with a Panama hat, strolled from the Ossler house up the drive to the road and along the grassed verge to the neighbouring property.

This house, he found, pleased him in much the same

15

areas that the Ossler house didn't strike his fancy. In the first place, it was old, early nineteenth century he thought, solid, centrally placed door, with a pane of frosted glass above to complete the door frame. There were windows at either side, first floor windows above that with a sash window above the doorway. As he drew closer he made out the date AD 1814 carved in stone in the wall beside the door. The garden in front of the house was a jumble of shrubs allowed to grow generously, with a narrow path of red brick which seemed to pick its way through the shrubs as though the latter had pride of place. The front garden was a place of blossom and bloom, and much insect activity. Hennessey reached the front door and found an old, possibly original, bell pull. He pulled it and heard bells jangle within the house. The door was opened a few seconds later by a young man with a mop of ginger hair, a cheesecloth shirt and a pair of faded denims. He smiled as he pondered the man who had presented on his doorstep, a man probably old in his eyes, lined features and mottled skin. "Police?"

"Didn't know it showed." Hennessey smiled, he glanced behind the man and saw children's toys lying scattered in the hallway.

"Doesn't really." The younger man returned the smile. "It's all the activity yonder. Can't miss it."

"Do you see much of your neighbour?"

"No. No we don't really. We don't socialise at all. If we see him, it's only in passing. Hear him a lot though."

"Interesting."

"Oh?"

"Sound."

"It is, isn't it? I prefer the radio to television for that

reason, the power of the human mind to imagine scenes is astounding, don't you think?"

"Oh yes, yes. I'm not a great one for television either." He nodded to the Ossler house. "What specifically did you hear from that house?"

"Noise, as opposed to sound."

"The difference being?"

"The difference as I see it is that noise is unpleasant to listen to, isn't orchestrated, tends to be emotionally led." He blinked against the sun and brushed away a wasp. "The difference between noise and sound is the difference between an argument and a piece of music."

"I follow you. And you heard noise from the Ossler's?"

"All the time, nothing but, even loud enough to carry across the distance that separates the houses and that's from within their house to within ours."

"What sort of noise?"

"Shouting, arguing, throughout the day and well into the evening, usually, in fact always his voice. His wife is a nervous, timid wee soul. Mind you, I've noticed this before or that before, overbearing men have timid, whimpering wives who'll do their husband's least bidding."

"Yes." Hennessey murmured. It was not an observation that he'd take issue with. Neither was the prevalence of over-bearing women with timid little Jack Sprats for husbands.

"It was always Ossler shouting, shouting at his wife, shouting at his secretary, shouting at someone on the phone, or so I presume, shouting at his dogs, poor beasts, a mad household and that's for sure."

"Did you hear anything last night from the Ossler house, I mean?"

"Dogs barking, but that's not unusual."

"Nothing else? Nothing out of the ordinary?"

"No . . . no, we didn't. I have good hearing, very sensitive ears, need spectacles for distance but my hearing is quite amazing, or so I've found over the years. Often, so often, I've heard things before people around me have heard it . . . you know ridiculed for hearing things and then a few moments later been proved that was exactly what I was doing, hearing things and doing so well before anyone else."

"But nothing out of the ordinary last night?"

"Not a dicky bird out of the ordinary, that is. I'd really like to help, sorry. What's happened anyway? Mind you I can guess, I've never known that house so quiet and I saw the black van drive away."

"You'd be right. You won't be hearing Mr Ossler shouting at anyone any more."

"You know, I'm not surprised. Not a man with friends, being my observation."

"So we're beginning to find out. The dogs, what time did you hear them barking?"

"Well . . . all the time really, they lived in a highly stressed household, they were nervous, jumpy dogs, clearly kept to bark and that's what they did. They got very little exercise, that tended to make them more irritable. They'll bark at anything, even a ringing telephone. But last night they were quiet for a while, barked at about ten p.m. or so."

"Ten p.m.?"

"About."

"No other sounds? The gate, the gravel?"

"The squeaky gate and the crunchy gravel? Again, no . . . again, I'm sorry. I'm sure I'd hear anybody walking on the

Osslers' drive. I hear the postman each morning. He calls to their house before ours. Ossler is self-employed and works from home and so he gets a lot of mail, calls about seven thirty each morning."

"Perhaps we ought to have a word with him?"

"I doubt he'd be able to tell you anything. He's a good lad, well on the ball. If he saw or noticed anything out of the ordinary he'd report it. Heard him come this morning, heard the gate creak, heard his footfall on the gravel, heard the dogs bark, they know him by the way, heard Ossler's letterbox snap shut a few times as he delivered their customary one ton of mail, heard him crunch back up the drive, open and close the gate, then a few moments later he drops our gas bill through our letterbox, delightful fellow. The next sound I heard was the cleaning lady's cycle and the dogs welcoming her. Then it was all hustle and bustle, and that doesn't happen in our village."

"Oh, but it does, Mr . . . ?"

"Locksmith."

"Are you self-employed, Mr Locksmith?"

"No. I teach at the university. Monday's a study day but this is the long vac . . . so I'm working at home. Don't do any teaching until term starts in October."

"Can't be bad."

"It doesn't mean that we stop work – that's a myth – lectures to prepare, lectures to update, my own research to continue. But it does mean that we can structure our own day, that's quite a bonus."

"I'll bet. So dogs at ten p.m. about, then silence until the dogs barked at the postman?"

"That's about it."

"It's a new house . . . Ossler's house?"

19

"Five years old. He bought the paddock, a three-acre paddock, got planning permission, planted that thing there. Confess the name amuses me."

"Thundercliffe Grange?"

"Yes. Hardly original."

"It rings bells."

"Wuthering Heights."

"Of course."

"It's such a naked . . . such a transparent copy but that didn't seem to bother Mr Ossler. Dare say he took a fancy to the name, decided to have it for his house. It might say a lot about him."

"Oh?"

"Well, my prejudice, naming a house in the first place, then copying a famous name . . . ah . . . Mrs Ossler."

Hennessey turned and watched as a police car drew up against the kerb in front of the front wall of the Ossler house. A slight-built woman in jeans got out of the front passenger seat. "She's quite young . . ."

"An awful lot younger than he is. They've been taken for father and daughter before. How she stood for all that shouting, maybe she thought the good living he offered was worth it?"

"Well," Hennessey nodded his thanks to Locksmith, "we'll see what she says."

Two

In which Hennessey meets a most youthful widow, learns more about the deceased and is intrigued by a telephone call.

I t wasn't until Hennessey stood close to Mrs Ossler that he realised how much younger than her husband she actually was. He could see what Mr Locksmith, their neighbour, had meant when he reported that they had on occasion been taken for father and daughter. He was also aware that many men fantasise about having a younger wife, though it was not a fantasy he had ever subscribed to, preferring the company of his own generation, and just then he did not at all envy Ossler his wife, despite her youth and good looks, if a little waifish, he thought. "Mrs Ossler?" he said gently. "I'm very sorry."

"Yes . . . what has happened?" Her voice faltered, her body trembled, she shivered despite the June warmth, her complexion seemed drained of colour.

"I'm sorry, I thought you'd been told. Mrs Ossler, I regret that I have to inform you that there has been an incident in your home, that a man we believe to be your husband is deceased."

"Oh . . ." She swayed a little, Hennessey held her by the

arm and felt only, it seemed, a bag of bones, waifish he
thought was perhaps right, her clothing probably covered a
woman who was verging on the anorexic.

"We can't talk here." Hennessey raised a hand, a constable approached. "Can you take this lady to the police
station?" He then turned to Mrs Ossler. "I'll have a chat
with you there. My name is Hennessey. Chief Inspector
Hennessey."

Mrs Ossler nodded, repeating his name and rank as if
committing it to memory amid the confusion. She allowed
herself to be escorted to a police car and was driven away.

Hennessey remained until the Scenes of Crime Officers had completed their tasks and he then familiarised
himself with the layout of the house; the small office
where the murder had taken place, a second small office
or study, the master bedroom upstairs, two further bedrooms
downstairs, the dining-room, the sitting-room, hallway, cup-
boards, kitchen, scullery. All very neat, and new, and as
he first observed, all very "just so". He went outside and
being a dog lover and owner, checked that the Alsatians
had sufficient water but kept them in the shed for fear that
they would contaminate the crime scene. He surveyed the
rear garden, the undisturbed neatness, the high fencing;
and then the front of the house to the lane, again neat,
again undisturbed. It all reinforced the impression if not
the certainty that at about ten p.m. the previous evening,
just over twelve hours earlier, some person or persons had
silently approached the house, gained entry, if not let in,
had coerced Ossler, or had been invited by him to the office
where he or she or they had shot Ossler once, blowing away
the front of his skull from the eye-line upwards. They
had then departed equally silently. Despite gravel. Despite

dogs. Puzzled, he drove the ten miles back to York, and to Micklegate Bar Police Station.

Mrs Ossler sat waiting for him in an interview room, she clutched a sodden handkerchief in one hand, the other was cupped round a plastic beaker, which contained the remains of vending machine liquid. Moving gently, being as least threatening in his body language as he could, George Hennessey sat opposite her and smiled gently. She returned his smile, a little forced he thought, but at least she did smile. She was, he reminded himself, more of a girl than a woman, more of a girl than a widow.

"It's a bad day for you, Mrs Ossler."

"Aye . . ."

"I'll try and make this as brief as possible."

"It's the sixth of June," she said looking at the Police Mutual calendar on the wall, "D-Day."

"So it is."

"I've been sitting here thinking that there's something significant about this date and that's it. It's the anniversary of D-Day."

Hennessey smiled. She was a woman in shock. The world about her would have an unreal, dreamlike quality. He'd been there himself, twice, he realised. He was twice bereaved and recalled the numbing "this isn't happening" feeling. He could well sympathise with her.

"Dead, you say? How?"

"He was shot."

"Shot! That doesn't happen in England."

"Oh, but it does I'm afraid. And with increasing frequency."

"Shot . . ."

"It's not a very English way of death, but it's death and

23

it's murder. And in all murder cases, the first twenty-four hours are the most important. So you've got to try and help us, Mrs Ossler. I know things are difficult for you, but you have to answer some questions."

"I'll try."

"Good." Hennessey opened a notepad and took the top off his ballpoint.

"I thought you tape-recorded interviews these days?"

"It isn't an interview in that sense. You are not a suspect. This could just as easily take place in your home or anywhere else that's convenient. Right now, the only convenient place is just here."

"I see."

"We've got to identify the victim."

"It's not my husband?"

"There's ninety-nine chances in one hundred that it is, but the gunshot wounds would make identification of the body . . . well, a little difficult. We've got to use other methods."

"Such as?"

"Well, was there likely to have been any other adult male in the home last night, or really at any other time?"

"No, not at any time, in fact. We hardly had any visitors."

"Your husband works from home, I believe?"

"Yes, most of his work is done on the phone or by mail. He doesn't like people calling, he's set in his ways."

"All right." Hennessey paused. "There are quite a few questions we have to ask . . . if it gets too much, just let me know."

Mrs Ossler nodded. "I'm fine, it's good to talk . . . if I was by myself . . . I don't know what I'd do, drink myself stupid I dare say."

"Well, try to avoid that, for your sake. Alcohol is a false friend, solves nothing. Makes things worse, in fact. But your husband, does he have a tattoo?"

"Left arm. Just here." She tapped her left forearm.

"Can you describe it?"

"A naked woman, what else? He had it done when he was very young and grew to be embarrassed about it. It's a woman, particularly large breasted and long legged, one hand behind her head, the other on her hip."

Hennessey drew a sharp breath.

"So it is him?"

"That description perfectly fits the tattoo observed on the deceased."

"Will you confirm it by checking his prints?"

Hennessey raised his eyebrows. "So, we will know him? We're doing a CR check as a matter of course but it's useful to know that we're going to get a result."

"CR?"

"Criminal Records."

"Yes, you'll have his fingerprints filed away. He got drunk once and told me he had a record. Nathan Hugh Ossler is his name."

"Any aliases?"

"None that I am aware of."

"Date of birth?"

"Well, he's fifty-six, March the first . . . you can work out the date of birth."

"Easily. What offences has he committed?"

"Fraud, lately. When he was a youngster he was convicted for rowdy behaviour, drunk and disorderly, that sort of thing."

"Dare say we'll find out. Is there anyone you can stay

with for the next day or two? You'll have to get the house cleaned."

"Cleaned?"

"Well, there's still blood on the wall of the room where he was shot."

"Oh . . ."

"The police won't clean that. That's up to the house-holder."

"I see."

"My brother. I suppose I could go back there. He'll let me keep the dogs . . . oh . . ."

"They're fine. They're in the shed, plenty of water."

"The shed?"

"If there was no family about we'd have taken them to the kennels we use in such circumstances."

"I see."

"Couldn't let them in the house, the house is still a crime scene. They've plenty of water and the window's open. There's also a constable in attendance. They'll be fine for an hour or two yet."

"Thanks . . . if Shane doesn't want them I suppose the kennels are the answer for a day or two."

"So, you were with your brother last night?"

"Yes, aye . . . Nathan won't have Shane near the house." She paused and glanced at the floor. "Wouldn't have him near the house."

"Was there bad blood between your late husband and your brother?"

"No . . ." she shook her head, "my brother, Shane, he's made his peace offerings, he's built his part of the bridge, but Nathan wouldn't have anything to do with him, says he's a ne'er-do-well, a tearaway. Nathan said that he rescued me from all that, but Shane would pull me back. Shane reckoned it was because he reminded Nathan of what he himself was like at the same age and so Nathan didn't like him.

"That's perceptive of your brother."

Mrs Ossler smiled. "That's Shane. He's got more about him than folk will give him credit for. Anyway, that was the set-up. I could visit Shane, but Shane couldn't visit me. So that's where I was this weekend, with my brother in York."

"All weekend?"

"From Saturday lunch time until this morning. I was collected this morning by the police officer but I was due back today anyway."

"Unusual, isn't it?"

"What is?"

"Well, you'll forgive me but when folk usually visit for the weekend they usually depart on the Sunday to be at home on Monday morning."

"No reason for me to return on the Sunday, always return on the Monday. No job for my hubby to be packed off to, no children to get off to school."

"Fair enough. Your husband won't collect you then?"

"Won't deliver me either. Such is his disapproval of Shanc. Or was his disapproval of Shane. It's lucky I get my monthly visit. First weekend of the month, that's the agreement. On Nathan's say-so: that would be a better way of putting it."

"I see. Sorry . . . your Christian name is?"

"Sadie. Sadie and Shane. Our parents didn't put a great deal of thought into our names, first ones that came to mind I reckon. I'd like to have had a classy name like . . . Anthea, Clarissa . . . and I would have liked Shane to have a sensible name. Shane, it's like a cowboy's name, a name like John. What's your first name, Mr Hennessey?"

"George."

"That's a good solid name. Shane could have done with a name like that. He's a good solid character. But Sadie . . . it's sad. Poor, sad Sadie."

"Sad Sadie?"

"It's what I got at school. Our parents didn't have a lot of money. Thank God for the charity shops. Sad Sadie, the cast-off kid. Eventually we got put into a children's home."

"That's school life. Those wounds never heal."

"You had similar experiences?"

"No," Hennessey grimaced. "No, I gave it out. To my endless regret and guilt. But we digress. So, you remained in your brother's company over the weekend?"

"Yes."

"In his house?"

"We went into York. Drinking most of the time in the Brown Bear. Touching base see, smoking fags, drinking beer, talking about motorbikes, it's the class of folk I belong to, I need that once a month as much as I need to see our Shane."

"That's useful," Hennessey smiled. "Neither you nor your brother are suspects but all that corroboration, all those witnesses to your presence, it means you're both well out of the frame. We'll still have to see your brother though."

"You will?"

"Yes. Just procedure. Don't be alarmed. Are you alarmed?"

"No, not about this, it's just our Shane . . . he's done a few daft things, he doesn't like the police, he's a biker."

"I see. Well we won't take his attitude personally. You feeling tired? How about a coffee?"

They sat in silence drinking the vending-machine coffee.

28

Hennessey broke the silence by saying that "this stuff" always reminded him of ersatz coffee. Sadie Ossler asked him what "ersatz" coffee was and so Hennessey told her.

"So tell me about your husband," Hennessey asked her when they had both tossed their empty plastic cups into the wastepaper bin, though not before Sadie Ossler had torn hers from rim to base into a series of narrow strips.

"What else can I say? He was all right. All bark really, no actual violence. If I'm not grief-stricken it's because I didn't love him." She looked up and held eye contact with Hennessey. "I didn't, I just didn't love him. That's it. There are marriages and there are marriages and somewhere out there, there might actually be two people who do really love each other but me and Nathan, we were not the two."

"Probably makes you similar to the majority."

"You think? I thought it was just me and him."

"Mrs Ossler . . . Sadie . . . I am shortly to retire and I have been a police officer pretty well all my working life. It's a job which is better than working and teaches you about life and I can tell you that the distribution of love, sex and money are identical: at any one time, the great majority of any or all is enjoyed by the absolute minority of people."

Sadie Ossler smiled. "I like that. I'll tell Shane and his mates, they're always going on about not having enough dosh. Yeah, they'll like that, it'll earn me a laugh and make them feel better."

"So, your marriage?"

"Well, he was a lot older than me, he bought me like he buys all his possessions . . . me . . . my job is to be there and look the part, rich man with his plaything, and this . . ." she tapped her ring, "this makes me a prisoner. I would have been better off being his mistress. I could have walked out at any time then. But the living was good. Like I said, I come from poverty so money means a lot to the likes of me. It's not so much the good things in life, the house, the BMW, the jewellery, it was knowing that with Nathan I'd never have to go hungry again. I'd help Shane out that way. Used to take a big bag of stuff each time I visited him."

"Stuff?"

"Food, as much non-perishable as I could carry, which is always the heaviest, tins and the like. Helped Shane to keep going. But Nathan, not an easy man to live with."

"Oh?

"He drank for one thing. I mean drinks, capital 'D', not like the pints me and Shane's mates drink, but spirits, vodka mainly, that's his tipple. He'd got a bit old, see, he wasn't interested in sex. We've been married for three years and I can count on the fingers of my hands . . . well I've got to a state where I don't miss it. I realised straight away what sort of man I'd married. He would show me off, he wasn't really interested in me or my body but I looked the part and that was that. Showed me off like a trophy, when he did bother to take me out. But we survived as a sort of couple. Him in his room, me in mine."

"Separate bedrooms?"

"Better that way. Having to share a bed with him . . . ugh . . . It's more honest."

"I can understand that. On a wider basis, would you say that your husband was a popular man?"

"Definitely not. Believe me, the world hated Nathan Ossler. Even his own son hates him."

"He's got a son?"

"From his previous marriage. There's no contact between

them. He's a grown man now, older than me in fact. My stepson is older than me."

"Do you have his address?"

"At home. He lives close by, Selby, in fact."

"Ah, yes, delightful town. But we'll have to have his address."

"Well, if you'll take me home, I'll let you have it. I can pick some things up, collect the dogs . . . would you mind . . . the dogs I mean?"

"Not at all. Your brother won't mind them?"

"No, he . . ." She seemed to be about to say something, checked herself and then said no, he wouldn't mind. But the way she stopped herself in mid-sentence registered with George Hennessey.

"Back to your husband . . . and the issue of his popularity, or lack of same."

"Well, he had a fight in the golf clubhouse last week, or the week before."

"Oh?"

"Had an argument with a lady, the wife of another member, poured his drink down her front and I mean down her front, down her cleavage. Her husband attacked him but Nathan was a match for him. It was like a bar brawl that you see in western films, other members separated them but Nathan was clearly the guilty party and was booted out. Didn't bother him though, didn't let it show if it did. I was there, I just wanted the earth to swallow me up."

"What was the name of the man and wife whom he assaulted."

"Hargrave. Richard and Thom."

Hennessey glanced at her. "Richard and Tom?"

"T. h. o. m." she smiled. "Thomasina."

"Ah . . . we have the Western Isles culture to thank for that. The traditional practice on Skye and points west and north is to name the boy before he's born and if it should not be a 'he' then the name still applies with an 'a' tagged on to the end, so we have Edwina's and Thomasina's and the like. Do you know their address?"

"No."

"No matter. A phone call to the secretary of . . . ?"

"The York and District Ancient."

"Expensive."

"The most expensive north of the Humber and south of the Tyne. So they say."

"The issue of your husband's popularity . . . what I'm driving at is, do you know, off hand, of anybody who'd want to murder your husband?"

"Not off hand. But from what I found out there'd be folk queuing up to shoot him. His first wife was murdered, did you know that?"

A pause. A silence. Then Hennessey said, "I didn't know that."

"Shot. Funny that."

"I didn't know that either."

"Not an English way of death, as you said, but it happened to both husband and wife, both at home too. I suppose that there is such a thing as coincidence after all."

"You'd better believe it. But tell me more."

"You know all about it. It happened here in York. About eight years ago."

Hennessey sat back in this chair. "*That* murder?"

"Shot on the doorstep. All I know is what he told me. Had a townhouse then, narrow-fronted but very deep, about two hundred years old . . . no front garden, though, front door opened on to the pavement, down a few steps, but on to the pavement."

"Yes, I know the type of house . . . you can sit in your front room and the only thing that separates you from the foot passengers on the pavement is a pane of glass. Lovely houses, though."

"Anyway, he had a duffle-coat he was fond of wearing, only he wore it, so he told me, except once . . . his wife grabbed it, she was just nipping out for a couple of minutes, it was raining, night time as well . . . his coat was hanging in the hall and rather than go upstairs to get hers—"

"Understandable."

"Aye. So she puts it on, puts up the cowl to cover her head against the rain, opened the door—"

"And was shot. I remember the case now. Dark, rainy night, nobody about . . . drew a blank on it."

"Scared Nathan. Sold that house and had Thundercliffe Grange built, fenced garden, rose trees, squeaky gates and gravel."

"And the dogs."

"Yes. Nathan wasn't going to sit like a coconut on a shy after that. It was clear to him that he was the intended target. Looks like somebody got it right this time."

"Certainly does." Hennessey absent-mindedly cleaned the end of his pen. "What line of work is your husband in?"

"Making money."

"Specifically?"

"Making money. I mean it. He had no skill, no one business, no expert knowledge. But if he saw an opportunity to turn a profit, he'd be right in there. If something was being sold beneath its true value Nathan would buy it, be it a piece of property or an antique."

"All legal?"

"Now you're asking, Mr Hennessey. I know he has convictions and so it wouldn't surprise me if my husband was a crook, but I didn't get to know anything. I was just there to look the part, like I said."

Hennessey said he'd take Sadie Ossler back to her house. He asked that she wait for him in the foyer and escorted her there. He walked back down the narrow parquet-floored corridor to his office, picked up the phone and jabbed a four-figure internal number. "Collator? Good. DCI Hennessey. There was murder in York, about eight years ago, lady by the name of Ossler . . . that's Ossler . . . file on my desk as soon as. Thanks."

Hennessey and Sadie Ossler sat in silence during the drive from Micklegate Bar Police Station to Strensall, and Thundercliffe Grange, still with the blue and white tape strung across the gate, still with the young constable in his summer tunic standing at the gate.

"How long will he be there, he or any police officer?" Sadie Ossler asked. "I mean, for his sake?"

"Dare say we could stand him down now, but we'll keep a presence until dusk. I think if nothing else, it does emphasise to the public that the house is a crime scene and that the police are in possession of it."

They left the car and walked to the gate of the house, Hennessey receiving a salute from the constable as they approached. They ducked under the tape, Sadie Ossler opening the gate with the usual accompanying squeak. She crunched the gravel until she passed the rose bed and then side-stepped onto the lawn. Following close behind, Hennessey did the same.

"Makes such a racket," Sadie Ossler said as the dogs

barked. "I used to ask Nathan why he didn't put a fence between the drive and the lawn to stop people walking on the lawn, never did get an answer. Nathan knew best you see. Even our postman does it, if he's feeling thoughtful."

"He gets past the dogs?"

"They know him. Nathan decided it was a risk worth taking to introduce them, otherwise he'd never get any mail. All right if I let the dogs out of the shed?"

Hennessey said yes, it would be all right but he'd be obliged if they were kept from going into the house. Sadie Ossler opened the shed door and the dogs welcomed her and then darted on to the back lawn of the house. Then she led Hennessey into the house. She walked through the kitchen to the corridor, past the room in which her husband was shot and entered a second room which was also clearly devoted to the pursuit of business.

"This is his study," she said, "as opposed to the typing room where he was found."

"The study." Hennessey looked about him, neatly kept desk and filing cabinet. No decoration at all. Anywhere.

"If the address book is in the house, it's going to be here. I'll leave you to look for it if you like?"

"I'd appreciate it." Hennessey began to rummage through the drawers, totally absorbed with his task, and then looked up and out of the window to the rear aspect of the house and saw Sadie Ossler with the dogs and saw her, glimpsed her by her body language, as a little girl with her pets. She seemed quite out of her depth with all that was going on around her, and in herself, not really, it seemed to Hennessey, to be in touch with the enormity of what had befallen her. She wanted only to play with her dogs. Returning his attention to the room, Hennessey noticed a telephone on the desk and on impulse picked it up and dialled 1471. He was told that a number which he wrote down as it was being dictated, had phoned the Ossler house on Friday last at nineteen thirty hours. He dialled the number. His call was answered promptly, a cheery female voice said, "Good morning, Crosshill School."

"Crosshill School?"

"Yes, sir. Can I help you?"

"Could you give me the address of the school?"

"I could. To whom am I speaking?"

"The police."

"Oh . . ." The telephonist then gave an address in Selby.

"What sort of school is Crosshill?" he asked as he wrote the address down, at the same moment catching sight of the waif-like Sadie Ossler throwing a yellow ball for her dogs to run after.

"A comprehensive school."

"No residents then?"

"No, sir. It's not a boarding-school or anything like that."

"I see . . . so, if a telephone call was made from the school at seven thirty in the evening, who would have made it do you think?"

"It could only have been one of the teaching staff, they often work late rather than take their marking home. The caretaker would be around then, checking the building, but he has his own phone in his house, it's a different number to this one. Mr Eddons might be able to tell you who was here. That's the caretaker."

"Mr Eddons. He has accommodation in the grounds of the school?"

"Yes, sir. I'm looking at his house now, it's across

the car park from the admin block where I am speaking from."

"Well thanks very much." Hennessey replaced the phone and then sat in the chair, reading the room. The room was neat, well ordered, everything in its place. Very, very functional, yet it had something "showy" about it, an office for the sake of appearances. The filing cabinet contained files with company names and also individuals' names, but mainly they were the names of companies. Small, one-man or family operations, it seemed, and the files themselves were balance sheets, mainly, it seemed to Hennessey, of money owed to Ossler. Mr Ten Per Cent indeed. He left the room undisturbed, closing the door behind him, but he knew intuitively that he'd return there.

He went up the spiral staircase to the master bedroom. Nathan Ossler's bedroom. Like the study, the room was neat and very functional. Not a room, Hennessey felt, that he could relax in. It contained a double bed, king-sized, sitting on a fitted carpet of dark blue. The bedroom had windows which looked out over both aspects of the property. From one window Hennessey saw the drive, the constable in his white shirt and blue trousers on duty at the gate, his car, a few houses. Turning the other way, he saw the green and yellow patchwork of the Vale of York stretching to a wide horizon under a blue sky. Again, the "everything in its place" aspect was what Hennessey absorbed most deeply. Ossler was a man who controlled all about him. The bedroom and the study also served to reinforce Yellich's notion that Ossler both knew and trusted his killer. Yet, there was also the emerging picture of a man with few friends.

"It doesn't add up," Hennessey said, speaking to himself.

"It just doesn't add up at all." But he found the address book and pocketed it.

During the journey back to York, with the dogs mute and curious in the rear seat of Hennessey's car, he said, "Did you call your husband at all over the weekend?"

"Yes," said Sadie Ossler.

Hennessey's heart sank. "You did?"

"On Sunday, just to confirm that I'd be arriving back home on . . . well today. That was about eight o'clock. Caught him in the pub."

"In the pub?"

"Yes. He strolled down to the White Hart on Sunday evening."

"He has a mobile?" Hennessey breathed more freely.

"Yes. He prefers it. Dead lazy if you ask me. Doesn't have to get up and answer the phone. Why do you ask?"

"Oh, no reason, no reason at all." He paused. "I've found the address book, it has Oliver Ossler's name and address. Would you like us to notify him of his father's death?"

"If you would. I'd like him to arrange the funeral. I don't feel up to it."

"I'm sure he would."

Hennessey drove Sadie Ossler to her brother's house on the Tang Hall Estate. She let herself and the dogs into the house. It was, thought Hennessey, a considerable fall from social grace to come from Strensall to Tang Hall, but he further observed that she seemed more at home in Tang Hall than at Thundercliffe Grange, and seemed eager to enter her brother's modest council house. Hennessey drove back to Micklegate Bar Police Station, wrote up his morning's work in the Nathan Ossler file and then walked the walls to Lendal Bridge and a late lunch in the fish restaurant.

After lunch he retraced his steps and enjoyed the cityscape with its sensitive blend of ancient and modern. An observer would see a tall, silver-haired man, of wise countenance, light stepping, with an expression of pre-occupation and puzzlement.

Three

In which Sergeant Yellich meets an iron lady and Hennessey a fallen Scoutmaster.

"To be honest, I don't know why either of them put up with him. Don't know why I did either, really." Sophie Asquith sat in a small upholstered chair beside the summer empty fire grate. At the further side of the hearth, a large pile of faded and musty-smelling newspapers had been allowed to accumulate. Sophie Asquith, so far as Yellich could tell, was not a smoker, no ashtray in evidence, her breath did not smell of stale cigarette smoke, yet the mirror above the hearth was nicotine stained, as was the ceiling of the room. It seemed strange to Yellich that a cleaning lady could live in such grubby surroundings. "He led both of them a dog's life."

"Tell me about him, or them."

"Always shouting, foul-tempered, foul-mouthed individual. She . . . his wife, had the worst of it, poor little thing, cowed like a rabbit she was most of the time. His secretary got a lot of stick too. His secretary could walk out more easily than his wife but she stayed just the same, despite all the rantings and ravings."

"How long did you work for him?"

"About a year . . . aye . . . it'll be a year this July. I wasn't planning on 'doing' for him for too much longer, people don't stay long with Ossler. I wasn't going to be an exception." She looked beyond Yellich at the garden of her cottage, outside the window. She had, noted Yellich, difficulty, apparently, in holding eye contact as she spoke, though her mind was clearly focused. "I didn't like the house. It had a bad atmosphere. I don't mean spirits or ghosts or such but I mean a bad feeling, like violence was about to erupt."

"Stressed? Tense?"

"That's a good way of putting it I think, I've been cleaning folks' houses all my days and you get the feel of good houses and bad houses. You get houses that are just warm. Even in winter they're warm. Stepping into them is like stepping out of a snow storm and into a summer's day, a day like today. Others are just cold. One house I did, cleaned for a gentleman who lived alone, had a key to let myself in and I was always pleased to leave it, it had a bad atmosphere. I could tell something awful had happened in that house . . . nothing to do with the man I cleaned for . . . but whatever had happened had left an atmosphere. Ossler's house though, there the bad is in the present, today, not hung over. Has to be, if only because the house is brand-new anyway. Only Ossler has ever lived there."

"Did you see anything unusual this morning?"

"Yes . . . yes . . . I did as a matter of fact."

"Oh?" Yellich sat forward from his seat in an upright chair.

"I saw Nathan Ossler slumped in a chair with his brains blown out. That's unusual enough, for one day anyway."

"Apart from that?" Yellich, chastened, reclined into the chair.

"Can't say that I did, young man." Sophie Asquith shrugged. "Dogs were a bit subdued, now we know why, I should think."

"You didn't notice anything out of place, apart from Mr Ossler's brains, I mean?"

"No . . . just the silence. It was as silent as a morgue, suppose it had become a morgue, hadn't it? I mean, in a way."

"He made it worth my while." Rosie Knott was a finely built young woman, but Yellich rapidly found that she was also a young woman who was made of steel. Her home had an "everything in its place" neatness which while on the one hand was a pleasant contrast to the mess of Sophie Asquith's home life, it also unnerved him for some reason. The photograph on the mantelpiece of a young man and a younger Rosie Knott, outside a church – he a bridegroom, she a bride – spoke clearly of a marriage, the house told of a, so far, childless union. That bit was either not wanted at all, or still to come, so thought Yellich, and he wondered how the Knotts would take to a child. Their home, like the Osslers', was really no place for sticky fingers and a thing which smells of warm milk and vomit and makes a noise totally out of proportion to its size.

"I had to disable him," she smiled.

"Disable him?"

"Make him dependent on me. You see, once, when I was quite young, I was with my mother and she was talking to another woman who said she'd left her job because her boss made her life impossible. Then she'd got a call from her boss asking her to return because he needed her, but this woman wouldn't. I thought then that I'd go back but he'd have to pay me, really pay. I reckon I was about ten. Then lo' and behold, there was me about ten years later in that same position, working for a tyrant that made life difficult for the world around him, but I just let it wash over me until I knew his business inside out and exactly how it worked, and all the while his attitude was getting more and more unpleasant. I mean, being called a 'stupid bitch' was nothing. I mean that was nothing."

"Pleasant fella?"

"But I had a plan, see. I just kept telling myself that each time he opened his mouth he was working himself deeper and deeper into a hole. Then, after about a year, I walked out . . . right in the middle of him dictating a letter. I just stood up and walked out. He was gobsmacked, said I can't do that. I said. 'Just watch me, sunshine, I've had enough of your attitude.' Came home, had a quiet fortnight waiting for the phone to ring and it did ring fourteen days later. In that time he'd had a string of secretaries, some of whom walked out after a few hours, just couldn't take his manner. The longest lasting one stayed for three days before she ran out of his house in tears, so his wife told me. Anyway, I said I'd return but it would cost him. I held out for a four-fold increase in pay." She smiled and looked pleased with herself. "That was a sweet victory."

"I can imagine." Yellich momentarily pondered his lifestyle should his annual salary be quadrupled.

"A month's pay each week."

"Not bad."

"Helped our mortgage, it's a new mortgage, we're up to the hilt in debt. Paul works in a bank and he handled

43

the transactions. He decided that we'd keep our spending power the same and pay the extra to the mortgage. He said it's always far cheaper to pay off your mortgage as speedily as possible. Take twenty-five years over paying off the loan and you end up paying three times the cost of your house. All this isn't as expensive as it looks, a lot is second-hand. We're striving to pay off the mortgage in ten years."

"Do you plan a family?"

"Eventually. Kill the mortgage first."

Yellich suddenly recalled speaking to a psychologist who worked with delinquent girls and who had said any time, any time, give me girls with shaven heads and swastikas tattooed on their hands, with studs in their nose and tongue, with their leather jackets and Doc Marten boots, because those girls are quaking with fear inside. It's the quiet girls who don't decorate themselves in any way and look comfortable in female clothing, it's those girls who are not frightened, it's those girls who can kill. And sitting here in the modestly spaced front room of a new build house on the edge of Strensall was a slender young woman with no decoration at all, save a wedding ring, and looking comfortable in a simple scarlet dress and sensible shoes, who spoke matter-of-factly about the premeditated disabling and extortion of a tyrant and about "killing" the mortgage, then, then Yellich knew what the psychologist had meant.

"Dare say it's back to normal pay now. But I was on good money for a year. That's equivalent to four years' income. It made a difference, brought the repayments down. You married?"

"Yes."

"Children?"

"One."

"Nice. How old?"

"Four or twelve, depending on how you look at it."

"Oh . . . I'm sorry."

"No need to be, but this isn't about me."

"No . . . it's about Nathan who went to hell this morning, or wherever."

"Wherever. Where were you yesterday evening by the way?"

"Here, at home, with Paul. Dreading going to work today. Why, am I a suspect now?"

"No, no more than anybody else who knew him, but I don't think you'll be in the frame, in fact you have a motive for keeping him alive, I mean, four times the normal money."

"I wouldn't have been there much longer. Another six months, we thought."

"Tell me about Mr Ossler's business?"

"Businesses, either businesses or not at all. He seemed to have a lot of interests. I mean business interests. He had only one personal interest and that was money. And that was his business, if he had a single business, lending and then getting it back as soon as, at great interest rates. He put a lot of people out of work. Essentially, so far as I could tell, he'd lend money to people who couldn't secure a bank loan, but the rates would be steep, and he'd never lend more than the assets of the business he was extending to, so he'd force the debt and strip the assets. Get his money back, plus some, and put some small businessman out of work in the process. Not difficult to see why someone would want to shoot him, is it? He's not the most popular man in the Vale of York, but he seemed to thrive on being disliked."

"Always from home? I mean, did he always work from home?"

"Home and the airfield."

"The airfield?"

"An old wartime base, now it's a sort of industrial estate, Ossler has a building there."

"Do you know the address?"

She glanced at the ceiling. "Yes . . . thinks . . . give me a minute. I've typed up letters as though posted from there . . . Newlands, that's it. Newlands Industrial Estate, Elvington."

"Ah . . . I know it. Driven past it a few times. Do you know what he's got there?"

"I don't, to be honest. I only know he's got something there because I type letters as coming from that address. Fairly weird letters, no details, sort of menacing tone . . . 'the payment is due shortly' sort of letter, but payment for what is not mentioned. He files all the copies of those letters at the airfield unit."

"Anything that we should know about, either at his house or the airfield?"

"Anything shady, you mean?"

"In a word 'yes'."

"Nothing that I ever came across, he seemed to do a lot of work on his mobile, often taking himself out of earshot . . . or he'd get a call and say 'hang on, I'd better take this upstairs' and off he'd go." She shrugged her shoulders. "So perhaps there were a few shady deals going down, I didn't see any details, though."

"I see." Yellich nodded. "Smoke but no identifiable source of fire. What was his relationship with his wife like?"

"Non-existent. When Himself was out of the house, me and Sadie would steal a natter over coffee. Poor thing, some life she had . . . always reminded me of that phrase used in nuclear power, what is it? A 'half life'. She seemed to have a 'half life'. Not even that, but she put up with him, went to see her brother when she could. I think she was worried about him, getting in with a bad crowd . . . she'd give him money if she could, but Ossler was such a control freak, she had to account for every penny. But I've heard that, the wealthier you are, the less generous you are. But she and her brother are quite close. Grew up in a children's home, only ever had each other."

"I can understand that. Any idea how Ossler and his wife met?"

"Through a lonely hearts ad 'The Meeting Place' in the *Yorkshire Post*, I think. He placed the ad, she told me. Something along the lines of 'successful businessman seeks younger wife'. She saw his lifestyle and was swept off her feet. Married quickly, then she woke up to what she'd let herself into, that's how it seemed to me, but she never complained, not to me anyway. Just took one day at a time."

"Not unlike you in a sense, letting it all wash over you."

"Perhaps. Perhaps that's how she survived."

Hennessey walked the walls towards Micklegate Bar Police Station. It was, he had found, and as all citizens of York knew, a much easier way of traversing the city centre than walking the pavement. He glanced to his left and pondered the building that was the original railway station, built "within the walls" as the local expression has it, and glanced further afield at the slate grey expanse of crowded housing, whose roads defined narrow and ancient streets. He left the walls at Micklegate Bar as a short-lived summer drizzle fell. He entered the police station and walked down narrow corridors to his office, picked up the telephone as he sat at his desk. He tapped a four-figure internal number. "Collator?"

"Yes, sir." The response was rapid, snappy, efficient.

"Hennessey here. I'm back in the office now, as you can tell."

"The Ossler file? Yes, sir. Have it here."

"That's the file on Mrs Ossler's murder?"

"Yes, it is."

"Nathan Ossler, this morning's victim, he was also known to us apparently. He'll also have a file, probably cross-referred to his late wife."

"It is, sir. It has been extracted for your information."

"Good man." Hennessey replaced the phone and walked from his desk to the wall of his office where stood a small table and an electric kettle, a couple of mugs, some tea, some coffee, some powdered milk. His coffee was still too hot to drink when a cadet reverently tapped on his door holding the files.

"For me?" Hennessey asked.

"Yes, sir." The collator asked me to deliver them.

"Thanks, son." Hennessey took the files and leafed through them. Hers first, Olivia Ossler, hence perhaps the choice of Oliver for their first and subsequently only born, and which lady had been forty-two years old when she was shot and killed while she stood on the threshold of her Georgian townhouse home. The contents of her file were short, brief and to the point.

```
Victim:           Olivia Ossler 42 yrs
Cause of death:   Single gunshot to the chest
                  area
Perpetrator(s):   Not known
Witnesses:        None
Motive:           None identified
```

And that, to Hennessey's astonishment, was it. Essentially the remainder of the report, compiled by the now long-retired Detective Sergeant Tend whom, Hennessey recalled, had been a sergeant in Her Majesty's Forces for much longer than he had been a sergeant in the City of York Police, was essentially a repetition of the item-by-item information given on the first page. Hennessey recalled Tend with clarity, a man of military bearing, of a non-commissioned officer type, perfectly turned out, clipped, abrupt way of speaking, a style which clearly extended to his report writing. Tend did, however, offer the theory that Olivia Ossler, who like the present Mrs Ossler, was weak and retiring by all accounts, had been shot in mistake for Nathan Ossler. She had, after all, been wearing his coat with the cowl up over her head. Hennessey, who strove for high-mindedness in all things and who hated sarcasm could not resist muttering "Oh, very good, Sergeant Tend, very good." He read on but Ted Tend had offered no further information or insight.

Hennessey leaned back and sipped his rapidly cooling coffee. The possibilities in respect of Olivia Ossler's murder reduced to:

(1) The shooting was indiscriminate, a lone gunman with a grudge against the world seeking a victim. There was no premeditation and no personal motive. Olivia Ossler had just opened the door at the wrong time.

49

(2) That Ted Tend was correct; the shooting had been a deliberate attempt to murder Nathan Ossler. Either way, Olivia Ossler had just opened the door at the wrong time.

(3) If (2) is assumed, the murder was either connected to the murder of Nathan Ossler eight years later, or it wasn't.

Hennessey decided that for the present he would assume option (2). He'd keep an open mind about any connection between the two murders. It isn't easy to murder somebody. It is, in fact, very difficult. Many have fantasised about it, but fortunately only a few people have the necessary psychological make-up to carry through the act, so had observed George Hennessey, who had spent almost his entire working life as a police officer. And of those who do commit murder, the great majority become consumed with guilt. Eight years, Hennessey pondered, was a long time over which to connect two murders and he felt in his waters that the murder of Olivia Ossler would remain unsolved. What had probably happened is that the murderer of Mrs Ossler had terrified himself or herself, had become eaten up with guilt about not just taking a life, but the wrong life, and had disappeared into the ether, had managed to keep their own counsel, speaking only to a priest, if at all. But time, Hennessey had learned, is on the side of the police, there being no such thing as a statute of limitations in the UK. Things may yet be resolved about the murder of Olivia Ossler.

He laid the file on Mrs Ossler's murder on his desk and picked up the file on Nathan Ossler. Here, he found, was a man whose track record further reinforced Hennessey's growing conviction that he would have found it difficult to like Nathan Ossler had they met in life. Ossler had been in trouble with the law since he was fourteen when the Juvenile

Bench of Newbury Magistrates Court had deemed him to have been "in need of care and control" and sentenced him to six months at a detention centre, in Newbury, Berkshire. Hennessey pondered, so Ossler was not a man of this shire. He was also a man who had moved around the United Kingdom. He acquired a further conviction for "malicious damage" when he was sixteen and still at Newbury, for which he was fined ten pounds. A sentence which spoke of a crime of great malice, but little actual damage. He paid a further fine following a conviction for drunk and disorderly and then his track record developed its true flavour, or its "hum".

In Ossler's case, the "hum" of his track was filthy lucre, specifically dishonest means of acquiring same: non payment of tax, fraud, receiving stolen goods, that whilst living in London and for the last offence he received his first prison sentence of twelve months, of which he served nine months at Wormwood Scrubs. By which time he was twenty-five years old. There then occurred a quiet period during which he either was a reformed character or more likely, thought Hennessey, he avoided detection, until the age of thirty-three when he served three years at Full Sutton for insurance fraud. Hennessey stroked his chin. Three years for IF – that spoke of a large, a very large scam, which began to explain the prestigious Georgian townhouse and later the ludicrously named "Thundercliffe Grange" and the BMW. There occurred a second quiet period, or a period of non-detection, interrupted by a five-year stretch again in Full Sutton, this time for blackmail.

"Interesting." Hennessey spoke aloud. "That could be very interesting." If, Hennessey thought, Ossler had been playing games like that, it would explain why one person would want to shoot him but shoot his first wife by mistake, and why a second person would also want to shoot him, but this time get it right. If the two murders were connected, they were connected only in that two separate murderers were possessed of the same motivation. If that was the case, then, Hennessey mused, the first murderer disappears even further into the ether and into his or her own self-consuming guilt.

Hennessey made a second mug of instant coffee and then settled back in his chair and read the account of the blackmail which earned the deceased a five-year prison sentence, of which he served three years. A Scoutmaster had allowed himself to be photographed while naked amid a group of Scouts, also naked, in a wooded area by a lake. The photographs, still in the file, had a vague, poorly defined quality about them which, to Hennessey's untrained eye, spoke of a series of pictures taken with a telephoto lens. There was indication of different weather conditions, varying amounts of cloud cover for example, and different amounts of daylight which further spoke of the photographs being obtained with planning and premeditation over a period of time, not in a single opportunist manner. That, plus the massive blackmail demand of fifty thousand pounds probably explained the length of the prison sentence collected by Nathan Ossler. The Scoutmaster had, according to the report, done the sensible thing and gone straight to the police who had set up a "sting" and Ossler was arrested when he collected a brown paper parcel from the arranged drop site, the parcel containing nothing but bits of newspaper. The Scoutmaster was a man called Parrott, Jeremy, who then had an address in Tollerton, conveniently a short detour off the route of Hennessey's journey home. He made a note of the address. He would pay a call there later that day.

There was a brief, reverential tap on his door. Hennessey looked up, a beaming Sergeant Yellich stood in the door frame.

"You look pleased with yourself, Yellich."

"Aye, boss, got a result from the fingerprints of the corpse, it's Ossler all right. Never any doubt really, but now it's confirmed."

"I'll let Mrs Ossler know, that's two things for me to do this afternoon."

"Two?"

"Yes, I want to pay a call on a Scoutmaster. Did you manage to see the secretary and the cleaning lady?"

"Yes, boss. Both paint the same picture of Ossler; ill-tempered, foul-mouthed, both wondered at his wife's ability to stick with him. They didn't even sleep together, apparently a marriage of appearance rather than actuality. He kept her on a tight rein, his wife I mean, had an allowance and had to account for every penny. Allowed her a certain number of visits to see her brother in York, that sort of thing, a real control freak, but she accepted it. I get the impression that there is something quite juvenile about Sadie Ossler."

"There is." Hennessey laid the file down. "She's not the run-of-the mill businessman's wife, if there is a good woman behind the successful Nathan Ossler, it ain't Sadie. She couldn't stand up to him, more's the pity, because all bullies are the same, if you do stand up to them they lie on their backs wanting you to tickle their tummies. Any solid Yorkshire lass would have had Nathan Ossler jumping through hoops in no time . . . I believe he knew that, hence his choice of wife. He didn't need a good woman behind him because he wasn't a successful businessman, he was a successful criminal."

"Oh?"

"Fraud, blackmail . . ."

"Blackmail!"

"Yes, I picked up on that too, Yellich, being blackmailed is a very good reason to want to terminate someone's life with extreme prejudice. But anyway, what's for action? Now we have proof of ID we can proceed with the PM, I'll tee that up with Dr D'Acre."

"Right, boss."

"We don't have to do this, but Sadie Ossler being the limited person she appears to be, we will do it. I also said we would. Can you get a constable to visit the deceased's son, Oliver Ossler, and inform him of the death of his father?"

"Right, boss."

"It's getting on four p.m., we're both put in overtime but I want to ask you to do something else before you get off home. Can you check Sadie Ossler's alibi? She reckons she was drinking in the Brown Bear with her brother's friends on Sunday evening. Find out if she was, and find the brother's surname if you can. I doubt if he's registered to vote, otherwise we could look it up on the Voter's Roll."

"Will do. Are they in the frame?"

"No more than anyone else at the moment, but it's a wide frame. Too wide, I'd like to narrow it down."

Yellich drove the short distance from Micklegate Bar Police Station to the Tang Hall Estate on the south-eastern edge of York. He drove slowly through streets in which tough little street turks whiled away the long summer. He halted outside the address he'd been given as that of Sadie Ossler's brother. It was a small terraced house, recently built, of a one bedroom design, allocated to single people or childless couples. He left his car and walked up the narrow path between two patches of litter-strewn lawn and knocked on the front door, causing dogs to bark from within the small house. The door was flung open, aggressively, by a well-set, perhaps overweight, youth, dressed in a studded denim jacket and a T-shirt with a grinning skull on the front. His hands were heavily tattooed in a rough and ready manner – a pin with a ball of ink-soaked cotton wool on the tip – in that manner.

"What!" The youth thrust his face directly at Yellich's face. The two Alsatians leaped and twisted behind him.

"Police. Detective Sergeant Yellich. Is Sadie Ossler in, please?"

"She's asleep in the bedroom." He held both dogs by their collars.

"In your room?"

"Yes . . . yes. Just lying on my bed. Better for her than the couch."

"You're her brother? Shane . . . ?"

"Shane Widestreet."

"Widestreet?" Yellich fought hard to hide his amusement.

"Something wrong with that name?"

"Nothing. Nothing at all."

"I've got to like it. I'd rather be called Widestreet than Smith."

"Tell you the truth, I think I would. I've really called to let your sister know that we've identified her husband, so it won't be necessary to ask her to make a visual identification."

"She'll be grateful for that."

"You were with her last night?"

"All yesterday. Spent the day drinking. In the Brown Bear, lunchtime session, came back for food and then out again for the evening."

"The Brown Bear? I don't think I know that one."

"It's on the estate. End of the road, turn left."

"I see. Well, thanks anyway." Yellich turned and walked away. As he did so the door was shut with a firmness, a finality, which said the occupant of the house didn't like the police. That suited Yellich down to the ground. He got in his car and drove off to the end of the street and then left. The Brown Bear revealed itself to be a new, brick built pub, set back from the road amid a sea of concrete upon which few cars stood, this being Tang Hall. Yellich thought the name of the pub odd, it didn't gel with the building, as if plucked out of thin air and stuck on the pile of bricks, rather than speaking for the history of the pub, or of the surrounding area. Inside it was superficial, inexpensive and tacky, to Yellich's eye. The landlord was a grey-haired man with hard eyes and similar tattoos on his hands and arms to the tattoos worn by Shane Widestreet. An ex-biker, thought Yellich, and one able to command the respect of young bloods.

"Widestreet, yeah. He's a regular in here. Him and his mates. They were in Sunday, yesterday afternoon, early. Came back for a drink in the evening, a game of darts, left when the pub shut at ten thirty."

"Anything special about them yesterday?"

"Nothing at all. Just the same Shane and Sadie. Him so big and her so small, wouldn't think they were brother and sister, but they are. Grew up in a children's home he told me, looked out for each other and got quite close because of it. She married a big nob but didn't turn her back on her roots. I can respect that. Liked her lager and game of darts."

Hennessey drove north out of York on the A19 and turned off at the first sign towards Tollerton. Captain's Garth in Tollerton proved itself to be a cul-de-sac of modest semi-detached houses. Quietly suburban, yet in a rural setting, shops close by, yet fresh country air and a flat landscape providing skies. Hennessey pulled up outside number fourteen, walked up the drive and pressed the doorbell which rang the Westminster chimes.

"Police?" said the bald-headed man who opened the door wide.

"How can you tell?"

"You have that stamp about you. I hope there is no trouble?"

"I don't think there is, nothing that you need be worried about. I'm really here to pick your brains, Mr Parrott. I take it that you are Mr Parrott?"

"I am he. Please come in."

The Parrott house was kept neatly, except for a computer and a word-processor, which sat on a table in the middle of the living-room, from which flex seemed to run in all directions.

"Please take a seat." Parrott indicated a chair and he and Hennessey sat. "How can I help you?"

"It's Nathan Ossler."

Parrott's jaw set firm. "Not my favourite person."

"Well, he's not anyone's favourite person now, he was murdered last night."

"Murdered!"

"Shot. We didn't really doubt his identity, but it was

confirmed just before I left the police station to come here. It'll be on the early evening news now, we're certain."

"Well . . ." Parrott sat back on the settee. "How the mighty fall."

"Where were you yesterday evening, Mr Parrott?"

"Here, all evening. Me and my lady wife and our friend there." He pointed to the television.

"She'll confirm that?"

"If she has to. Why, am I a suspect? Confess if I am, it's taken me a long time to get round to doing what I've spent the last few years fantasising about doing. That man ruined my life."

"Rather ruined your own life I'd say. I've seen the photographs. They're still in his file."

"Well." Parrott sat forwards. "You know I'd say to you that there's more to those images than meets the eye. I still maintain that I did nothing wrong."

"Cavorting naked with a group of naked boys in a wood by a lake, that's a hard act to justify in this political climate."

"It's not exactly flavour of the month, I'll grant you, but I still didn't do anything wrong. You see, Mr . . ."

"Hennessey."

"Mr Hennessey, you see, Scouting was my life, I was a Scout, became a Scoutmaster, I lived for the Scouting movement . . . and there may well be a small amount of sexuality in the movement. The initiation of young Scouts fully into the movement at this first camp has its sexual overtones, but that's the way it is. That's the way it's always been, it's an important part of the bonding process. My wife, she was a Girl Guide, her father wasn't a rich man, she attended a tough comprehensive school, while most of the other Guides in her company were daughters of professionals. Yet she tells me that it was in the Guides that she really learned to drink and smoke and swear."

"I don't doubt it, but . . ."

"But what I want to tell you . . . well I want to tell you for my own sake, those photographs . . . it made me so angry. You see, I have no sexual interest in children whatsoever, my wife and I have a good sex life, but we're both naturists."

"Ah . . ."

"You see that's what I did wrong, if anything. I allowed the boundaries of the movement to merge with my own values. I didn't like this prissy covering up of 'private parts' so called. There's nothing wrong with the human form. Anyway, one day at a camp in the Lake District, a blistering, hot day, I peeled off my kit and dived into the water. The lads looked at each other and then they all did the same. I was so proud of them, maybe we were blundering into the sexuality of it, and maybe on that weekend I was a naturist instead of being a Scoutmaster, but nothing overtly sexual happened at all. I didn't touch them and they didn't touch me or each other, at least not that I was aware of."

"It happened only once?"

"No . . . no, it didn't. That very hot summer, it became a feature of the troop to go 'skinny dipping' at its own request. And boys talk. Rumour spread and I was eventually shown a series of photographs, a bit blurred, telephoto lens, must have been a real elephant gun. I later went and believe I found the vantage point used by the photographer; a quarter of a mile away across the lake and accessed by a steep slope, no track at all. It was a deliberate and determined ambush. Never did find out who took the photographs."

"Not Ossler?"

"No. He's too lazy." Parrott pulled a hand down over his

face. "What happened is that someone had possession or access to an elephant gun of a lens and took the photographs. There were week by week changes in the photographs. So someone knew when we were going where . . . you know the weekend we tried to build a raft, the only weekend that a particular boy came . . . someone watched us each weekend that we went away that summer. About four or five weekends all told. But whoever it was hadn't the bottle to go ahead with the blackmail and, so I suspect, sold the photographs and negatives to someone who was callous enough to blackmail."

"That person being Nathan Ossler."

"The one and the same. Ossler had a reputation. Long before I met him I had heard of him. The local villain, York and its region, the Vale . . . not a large population. It's not so easy to hide here, either yourself or your reputation."

"No anonymity?"

"Is a succinct way of putting it, Mr Hennessey." Parrott smiled. "I knew of Ossler by reputation, but the first time I met him was when he came here, walked in as though he owned my house, dropped the prints of the photographs on the table there and told me the negatives would cost . . . well, about the market value of my house. I mean, he and I may as well have been playing Monopoly. He then told me he was a professional blackmailer."

"He said that?"

"He did. He said that he was good at it, been doing if for years. The trick was, he said, to target someone who can't go to the police and to never ask for more than the victim could afford. He invited me to negotiate a second mortgage on the house and so raise the money; that way I'd keep my job. I'm a school teacher, primary, and I could still continue to 'enjoy' myself at weekends. He was smug and arrogant, though his language was choice. And I mean choice in the extreme."

"But you did go to the police."

"Yes, I did. The police took statements from the boys, no bad news. I made a statement to the school governors and kept my post, aided by letters of support from the organisers of the British Naturist Movement to the effect that both myself and Meg, my wife, are genuine naturists and have been so for many years. The Scouts were less accommodating, probably because I had no contract of employment with them as such. They said I'd been 'ill-advised' and 'indiscreet' and invited me to resign. I felt a bit like Captain Oates leaving the tent to walk to his death for the benefit of his companions. That is a very hard thing to do. To leave something that you've been part of for so long because by doing so, you make the only contribution you can make. I turned to drink for a while but got a hold of that in good time."

"Good for you."

"You know the mistake he made wasn't so much that he saw the photographs as evidence that I was a paedophile, but that he broke his own second rule, we just couldn't afford a second mortgage. If he'd asked for less, I might . . . just might have found the money."

"That's called mating with a scorpion. You'd never have got rid of him then."

"You're probably right, because the police set up a sting operation. After a few weeks I phoned him and he told me to have the money ready and that he'd bring the negatives with him . . . the phone conversation was being taped."

"I see."

"Told me he'd come to my house and collect it, which again suited the police because they installed hidden cameras in the house. Anyway, he came, picked up the suitcase, opened it, saw it contained newspapers and said 'Where's my money?', at which point the police made their presence known. The look on his face . . . it was a picture. But he didn't have the negatives with him. As you say, the price he asked was really just the first instalment. The police never did find the negatives, though now they're quite useless. But Ossler, clever man, knew when the game was up, went G to blackmail, collected five years, out in three with remission."

"And probably started again."

"You think?"

"I think so. This time he put the screws on someone who couldn't go to the police and so relieved him of his brains instead."

George Hennessey drove the short distance from Jim Parrott's house to his own house in nearby Easingwold. His house was a modest, inter-war four-bedroom detached house standing in generous grounds on the Thirsk Road. He let himself in the house and was warmly greeted by "Mick" a black crossbred who looked like a scaled down Labrador. Still patting his dog about the neck, he stooped to pick up his mail and then walked out into the rear garden because that's where his wife was. The lawns, the dividing privet, the pond, rich in amphibia, in the rough ground, or the 'going forth' as she had referred to it. Always, always at the end of a working day he came to the garden to say "hello" to Jennifer.

Later, after a meal, after he and Oscar had taken their customary evening stroll, Hennessey walked into Easingwold for a pint of stout. He enjoyed the beer, he enjoyed the conviviality of the pub, but more, he enjoyed the walk in the still, warm air under a vast, crimson sky.

It had not, he thought while on the return leg, been an unsuccessful day's work.

TUESDAY

Four

In which the gentle reader learns of the vulnerabilities of Yellich and Hennessey, and a suspect moves into the frame for the murder of Nathan Ossler.

F eeling energetic and knowing that his body, being elderly in terms of a policeman, was in much need of exercise, and it being a fine summer's morning, George Hennessey decided to walk from Micklegate Bar Police Station to York District Hospital. By reason of both preference and pragmatism, he chose to walk the walls as far as Lendal Bridge where once the working girls would stand before they were removed because it was bad for tourism, and who now all rent rooms in saunas, and walked up Museum Street, already bumper to bumper with open-topped tourist buses. He turned left and followed the graceful Georgian crescent which is St Leonard's Place. He crossed Bootham Bar and walked down Gillygate, of small, often interesting shops of the Victorian era, to Wiggington Road and to the grey, low-rise, slab-sided hospital. Walking across the car park his eyes swept from side to side, searching for a specific car and his heart leapt as he saw, utterly unmistakable, a red Riley with white mudguards and black roof, circa 1947 and in pristine condition. Only one like it in the Vale of York, if not the entire north of England. When he saw it, his pace quickened.

In the hospital he walked to the pathology department and to the office of Dr Louise D'Acre.

"Inspector Hennessey," Dr D'Acre smiled warmly. She was a slender woman in her forties, short cropped hair which was dark but greying here and there which Hennessey knew didn't bother her at all. He knew that she had three lovely teenage children and that her life was fulfilled. She did not fight the years, but grew old with grace and dignity and was much more attractive, in his eyes, because of it.

"Dr D'Acre, I saw your car in the car park. I knew you'd be in." He sat unbidden in a hard chair in front of her desk.

"Oh, so nobody's nicked it yet then?" she chuckled warmly.

"Nobody will, it's not re-saleable."

"Oh, but it is. My garage proprietor has advised me to have it alarmed and fitted with all sorts of fancy gadgets. Private collectors you see. If you can steal an original Van Gogh and find a buyer for it, nicking a 1947 Riley will not present an obstacle."

"I dare say, looking at it like that."

"It's the only way you can look at it. So what is for us today, one Ossler, Nathan believed to be?"

"Is . . . his identity was confirmed at close of play yesterday."

"ID confirmed." Dr D'Acre wrote on the medical record. "And was a sprightly fifty-seven years when he died in suspicious circumstances. Apparently by gunshot wound. Don't get many of those. Not in the Vale we don't."

"So people keep observing."

"Well, shall we have a look at him?"

In the post-mortem laboratory, Hennessey and Dr D'Acre both dressed in green coveralls and wearing latex gloves, stood back to allow the medical photographer to photograph the injury sustained by Nathan Ossler, who, clothing removed, revealed himself to have been, when alive, lean and muscular. The medical photographer took a series of photographs of the injury from every angle and then stepped back and smiled at Dr D'Acre. "All finished," she said.

"Thanks, Mary." Dr D'Acre stepped forwards and examined the wound. She spoke for the benefit of the microphone which was attached to an adjustable, stainless steel arm which protruded from the ceiling to a point above the steel table on which the body lay, and level with the top of the pathologist's head. "So the date is Tuesday, seventh of June, the time is . . ." She glanced at Hennessey who consulted his wristwatch and told her. ". . . oh nine forty-two in the forenoon. The post-mortem is in respect of one Nathan Ossler, aged fifty-seven years. Immediately obvious is massive trauma to the front of the skull consistent with gunshot wounding. The front of the skull has been removed by the trauma along with the frontal section of the brain which is quite unusual."

"It is?"

"I am not well versed in gunshot wounds, but most bullet wounds to the skull take the form of entry and exit wounds, such blowing away of the skull is quite unusual. What has happened here has been caused because the deceased has what is called an eggshell skull."

"A very thin skull?"

"That's it. Whatever else might have happened to him in life, he never banged his head. Anything that might

69

have given either you or me a headache or a lump on the head, would have killed him. It meant that the skull wasn't strong enough to withhold the shock waves that cause cavitation."

"You've lost me."

"Well," Dr D'Acre rested her hands on the side of the stainless-steel table. "Cavitation is the hole caused by the shock waves from the bullet. It's a temporary condition, the bullet pushes soft tissue away from it, both before it and beside it, causing a cavity measured in inches. The tissue falls back into place almost instantly, but in a very damaged form. Cavitation can be fatal, if the shock wave which causes the cavitation reaches a major organ, then death can result, even though the bullet didn't actually touch said organ."

"I see."

"In this case, the bullet entered the front of the skull, caused cavitation, but the thin nature of the skull meant it wasn't strong enough to contain the shock wave and the front of his head blew open. You didn't find the bullet did you?"

"No . . ."

"It's because it fragmented." Dr D'Acre took a pair of tweezers and extracted a minute sliver of metal from the brain tissue. She placed it in a small glass jar. "I'll recover as many of these as I can, see what a ballistics expert can make of them. But I've only come across this fragmentation effect once before and that was when the bullet concerned was a dumdum bullet, so called, small cuts in the top of the bullet cause lines of weakness. When the bullet is fired it causes it to explode on impact. Very messy indeed."

"As I see."

"Normally a bullet would have passed straight through the

skull, especially one as thin as this. But as you see, exploding bullet, thin skull . . . quite a mess. The calibre of the bullet was quite small, I would say a .22, which is a bullet that does its damage because of the sheer kinetic energy discharged on impact. They travel faster than any other bullet that can be fired from a handgun, but I'll have to refer you to a ballistics expert for authoritative interpretation."

"It was a handgun though, you think?"

"Only because I saw the scene of the crime, Chief Inspector. Difficult to see a rifle being used in such a confined space, or concealed from the road to the house. Just conjecture really."

"I wouldn't take issue with it," Hennessey grunted. "From the word go I had thought this a handgun number."

"Where would you get one from?"

"Ways and means, there's ways and means, but that's a good point. It means the culprit probably had some connection with the criminal fraternity. You can obtain a handgun in Britain but only if you know someone who knows someone."

"Very well . . . that's your department. The cause of death seems certain, but I'll trawl for poison as a matter of course. The airways are unblocked, there's no other noticeable injury, no discoloration of the face, which might suggest he was strangled before being shot . . . pupils . . . normal . . . I feel confident that the bullet terminated his existence. The angle of the trajectory, going by the remnants of the entry wound and the fact that the top and front of his head has been blown off, suggests that the gun was fired upwards into his skull from directly in front."

"A much shorter person?"

"Or someone sitting in a chair with the deceased standing

over them. But whatever, the angle of the bullet seems angled upwards, probably by about forty-five degrees."

"Time of death could be quite crucial for us."

"As always," Dr D'Acre smiled. "I noted the rectal temperature at the location, the time and the room temperature. I did some prep before you arrived this morning, using Henssge's nomogram method, and allowing for the fact that the deceased was clothed, I have arrived at a time of death nine to eleven hours before I arrived. I took the rectal temperature at nine thirty-two hours, and so I calculate a time window of about two hours from twenty-two thirty hours on the day before the body was found."

"From ten thirty on Sunday evening to half past midnight on the Monday forenoon." Hennessey mused. "I've worked with much wider time envelopes than that."

"I can't narrow it down any further I'm afraid."

"It's narrow enough."

"What might help is his last meal. Would you like to take a deep breath?" Dr D'Acre took a scalpel and made an incision above the stomach cavity, gases hissed as the stomach was punctured. She inclined her head to one side as the gasses escaped. "Never gets any easier," she said, forcing a smile. "But that wasn't so bad, quite a fresh corpse you see." She peeled back the layers of skin and peered into the stomach cavity. "Now this is interesting?"

"Oh?"

"Yes, he ate Indian and did so not more than one hour before he died."

"Bingo!"

"Naan bread, chicken tikka . . . in the main. He didn't masticate well, tended to swallow without chewing, not good for the digestion or extracting of protein . . . here you see bits of chicken tikka are still identifiable." She pierced a piece of meat with the scalpel and held it up for Hennessey's edification. "See?"

"That's interesting. You know, I can't see Ossler bothering to go out and eat, but I can see him sending out for a delivery. There'll only be one or two Indian restaurants that will offer a delivery service to a fairly remote village like Strensall . . . if we can obtain the time of that delivery . . ."

"You'll be able to narrow the time of death down further. He died within one hour of eating it. Anything from fifteen minutes to sixty minutes after eating it. That's a time window of forty-five minutes." Dr D'Acre continued. "My children have a passion for Indian food, we have home deliveries. Our local Indian restaurant won't deliver after eleven p.m., which is quite normal."

"So we are looking at time of death being nearer the beginning than the end of your time window, nearer ten thirty p.m. Sunday, than twelve thirty Monday, a.m.?"

"I would think so, Chief Inspector. I would think so."

"And shortly after he was shot with a single bullet which exploded on impact and popped his skull open because of the effect of . . . ?"

"Cavitation. A bullet doesn't so much push its way through solid flesh, it's more in keeping with flying through a near vacuum which is caused by the shock waves which the bullet pushes in front of it and around it. The faster the bullet, the greater the shock waves, hence the great damage done by the small .22 calibre weapons. A very small bullet, but oh, does it fly through the air."

"The track . . . the trajectory of the bullet was upwards?"

"At about forty-five degrees and, as I said, given the way

the deceased was slumped in the chair, I'd say that he was standing when shot. The murderer was much shorter than he or was sitting when the trigger was pulled." Dr D'Acre paused and turned her attention once again to the wound. "No gunpowder burns," she said. "Again, as previously mentioned."

"No what?"

"Gunpowder burns. It means that the muzzle of the gun was at least eighteen inches away from the entry wound. Ties in with someone sitting down in front of the deceased when the shot was fired."

"Pleasant way to spend a Sunday evening."

"Oh, I'm sure he didn't plan it like that." And Dr D'Acre and George Hennessey laughed, gently, but in deep enjoyment of each other's company.

"What now, boss?" Yellich asked.

For some reason that he could never fathom, but that he had long noted was a tendency of his, George Hennessey glanced at the clock on the wall of his office before answering: ten fifty in the forenoon. "Or who, or where?" he said. Then glanced out of the office window at a cloudless blue sky. "You know when it comes down to it, we know precious little more than we did this time yesterday. Nathan Ossler was shot on Sunday evening. That's it."

"Being unfair on yourself, boss," Yellich smiled, leaning forwards as he did so. "We're getting background on Ossler. One nasty piece of work, professional blackmailer did you say? If he's done it once, he'll do it again . . . and that's a very handy motive to bump someone off. He made a mistake with the Scoutmaster by all accounts, thought he'd caught a paedophile who couldn't go to the police, but if he learned from that mistake and was squeezing someone he had found who genuinely couldn't go to the police . . . then that's a strong motivation."

Hennessey smiled. "Keep talking to me, I'm beginning to see a road ahead. There *is* a path through the Great Grimpen Mire after all."

"No guarantees, boss, but that's how I'd be inclined to approach it."

"I think you're right. I don't think it's domestic . . . Mrs Ossler is well set up by the murder of her husband, but I think she'd prefer him alive to look after her and, anyway, her alibi checks out. I'm more puzzled by the phone call Ossler received from a school well after the school day had finished. I also want to talk to the guy who had a fight with Ossler at the golf clubhouse. There's a background there, more to it than Ossler insulting the man's wife by pouring beer down her front."

Yellich nodded. "There is, isn't there? Ponder it. What hold had Ossler over that fella that could enable him to do that in public? Has to be something."

"Has, hasn't it, Yellich?" Hennessey stroked his chin. "Right, I want you to go and have a look at his warehouse. Find what you find and then go and have a chat with Oliver Ossler. He's part of the network and he may or may not be involved, T.I.E., Yellich, T.I.E. trace, interview, eliminate. Talk to him, seek a motive, seek his whereabouts on Sunday last, two hours either side of midnight. Oliver Ossler is also likely to benefit from his father's murder but that may not amount to a motive. Much depends on the will and the contents therein, or what people believed to be the contents therein. Then I want you to go looking for an Indian restaurant."

"An Indian restaurant, boss?"

"Ossler's last meal was Indian, likely to have been delivered. Seek an Indian restaurant that will deliver in Strensall, see if they have a record of a delivery to Ossler's house on Sunday. If so, what time was it delivered? Dr D'Acre tells me that Ossler was cooled within thirty minutes of eating his last meal. Forty-five minutes at the outside. If we can find the time of that delivery, it will narrow the time of his death down nicely."

"Very good, boss."

"I'm going to have a chat with a couple of blokes if I can find them. Meet me back here at what time . . . ? Four p.m.?"

Yellich stood. "Four p.m., boss. Four p.m."

Crosshill Comprehensive School revealed itself to be an angular, flat-roofed, new-build building, light-coloured brick, concrete, metal-framed windows. Hennessey parked his car on the driveway outside the school buildings and walked, not to the school itself, but to the detached house which stood in the grounds, opposite the school, yet clearly of the same age as the school and clearly belonging to it. Clearly, thought Hennessey, clearly it was the caretaker's house. Clearly so.

"Best job I ever had." Bill Webster sat in the chair by the open hearth. The weather was too warm for a fire but the chair went with the hearth and Bill Webster went with the chair. He had a large, ruddy face, warm eyes, thought Hennessey. He seemed to smile a lot and sat with mottled hands clasped over a round stomach. A neat mantelpiece on which a framed sketch of a young soldier in tropical kit spoke of an existence before becoming the caretaker of

Crosshill Comprehensive School. "It's a holiday, see, Mr Hennessey, a real holiday. You swap your jobs and then you drop on one you like and it's a permanent holiday. School caretaker, lovely job, lovely. Get a house, this house, well apart, no rough estate for I. After five o'clock, or early in the morning and at weekends, well you'd think you're in the country. Are in a sense, badgers and foxes about, woodpeckers in the trees . . . my dog has the playing fields to romp on . . . lovely, lovely job."

"Lucky man."

"Aye, and I appreciate it. But it hasn't always been this way . . . I down shifted to get this job. Bet you don't know what I was once?"

"Tell me."

"Sales Manager for a large supermarket chain. The Vale of York was my patch, twenty branches. I had to keep the level of sales up to a quota. I had it all, flash company car, smart suits, expense account, all the patter, all the trappings, but I was working seventy hours a week and I was driving home one night and I thought 'what am I doing it for?' We had our children early in life, they're up and away. So I had a chat with Joyce . . . we'd paid off our mortgage, and had enough to see us out, so I took this job. Have to live in this house, so there's a presence on the grounds at night. Doesn't stop them breaking in from time to time, though."

"I'll bet."

"The drop in income looked a lot on paper, but in fact it's not been so different, and the outgoings are less. A big income leads to an expensive lifestyle. If you've got it you only spend it. This has been a very good move. A very good move indeed."

"Not bad." Hennessey was pleased for the man.

"Aye . . . get up early, me and my dog, open up for the cleaners, report any damage, mostly it's leaking roofs. Flat roof you see. They shrink. Flat roofs never work. Lock up in the evening after the cleaners have left and that's the job . . . just the job, as my old dad would have said, God rest him."

"So you'll see the early arrivals?"

"Aye. From time to time."

"And the late departures?" It suddenly occurred to Hennessey that apart from his facial muscles, Bill Webster hadn't moved at all since he and Hennessey began speaking, he had also avoided all eye contact. Odd trait, Hennessey thought, for a man who had been a manager in a large company, difficult to motivate people without eye contact, so Hennessey further thought, and had indeed found to be the case. "It's the late leavers I am particularly interested in."

"Well how late is late? I don't exactly stand a guard duty on the place."

"I appreciate that, but specifically Friday last at seven thirty p.m. about."

"Mr West." Webster smiled. "The Headmaster. I saw his car in the car park. Often do in fact. He tends to work late two or three evenings a week, doesn't like to take his work home. All the others get off a.s.a.p. with briefcases bulging with exercise books, marking for the purpose of, but Mr West once said to me 'home is home and work is work and the twain should never meet, if possible.' He's just not a home worker. I didn't use to be either, if I could help it but he has the advantage of his own office to work in. The other staff have to work in the staff room. To leave the school they have to pass through a set of fire doors, which are also alarmed. I have to lock those at six thirty each evening, so the staff have to leave by then, but Mr West and the deputy head have their own offices from which they can leave the school building via a side door, which isn't alarmed. There's nothing in his office or the deputy head's office or the secretary's office to attract burglars. All the computers and tape recorders in the language lab are on the first floor blocks and are wired up like the Bank of England. So I saw Mr West's car in the car park last Friday evening at about seven p.m. I took Jasper, my best friend, for a romp on the playing fields so as to walk round the buildings. Spent about an hour doing it and then returned to put my feet up for the evening, but when I passed the staff car park on my return it was empty. Mr West having gone home, I presume."

"Is Mr West in the school at the moment, do you know?"

"Well, he arrived this morning, looking spruce and snappy, all fine and dandy. If there's a blue Mercedes in the car park . . ."

"A Mercedes Benz?"

"I thought that as well when I saw it . . . but he told me that it was purchased second-hand and once you found the money for one, they're about the only car that will retain their value. And he also enjoys lots of street cred from the pupils owning one. A few more days and you'd have missed him for six weeks. He has a house in Brittany."

Hennessey raised an eyebrow. "A Mercedes Benz and a house in France – on a teacher's salary?"

"Same excuse as the Mercedes. The house in France was a very inexpensive purchase, but image is impressive. So he told me. His house here in the Vale isn't to be sniffed at either, so I'm told. Tell you the truth, I think he won the lottery. That would make more sense than a magical ability to stretch a coin of the realm further than any other known teacher in the state sector, living or dead."

Hennessey grinned. He enjoyed Webster's dry humour. But on a more serious note he, the police officer, began to feel his suspicions, honed by a life working among felons, becoming aroused. As Bill Webster said, a Mercedes Benz second-hand or not, plus two properties, isn't bad for a headmaster of a comprehensive school. Private means, Hennessey felt, were strongly starred. "And a six-week holiday each summer."

"They all say they need it. Probably do as well. I couldn't teach. Couldn't teach at all, but do you know where the tradition of the long summer holiday comes from?"

"I don't."

"From the days when the children were needed at harvest time. All hands, no matter how small, were needed to garner in the wheat fields until all was safely gathered in."

"Well," Hennessey stood. "You live and learn. I'll go and pay a call on Mr West."

"Happy to be of service, but you'd better mind your 'p's and 'q's, he's a very proper gentleman, top public school and Cambridge University."

"Very impressive."

"If you think so. Don't get many of his ilk in the public sector, though, dare say his social conscience is pricking him."

"It's been known." Hennessey said that he'd see himself out but Bill Webster still displayed no intention of moving any muscle, save those in his face.

Enjoying the heat of the midday sun on his face, George Hennessey walked from one flat-roofed building to another,

Perils and Dangers

from the caretaker's house to the school building. He walked up the steps of the school and pulled open a metal-framed glass doorway and entered the school, brown corridor, yellow painted plaster walls. A large sign in chalk on a portable blackboard read SILENCE EXAMS. He walked along the silent corridor until he found an alcove in which was set a door labelled STAFF ROOM. He stood for a moment in front of the door deciding how to knock and eventually chose to amuse himself, by knocking twice, timidly, at waist level. He waited for a moment and then the door was flung wide by a young teacher looking down, clearly, as Hennessey had hoped, expecting to be confronted by a quaking and quivering twelve-year-old. Hennessey enjoyed the look of surprise and shock on the teacher's face as he towered above the member of staff and said, "Hello. Police."

"Oh . . . yes?"

"Mr West, please."

"He'll be in his office. I'll show—"

"Directions will be fine, thank you."

Hennessey followed the directions given, which involved retracing his steps towards the main door of the school and walking beyond them, down a flight of steps to another alcove in which there were three doors, labelled SECRETARY, DEPUTY HEADMASTER and HEADMASTER. He tapped on the Headmaster's door. There was an imperious pause before a soft-spoken male voice said "Come".

Hennessey in turn, waited a very long, very imperious two, perhaps three seconds before entering the room on his terms. "Hello," he said to a shocked-looking Headmaster. "Police."

"Please," the smartly dressed man replied, "won't you sit down?"

Hennessey sat reading the room as he did so: small,

cramped, even, very neat. A framed aerial photograph of the Chapel of King's College, Cambridge hung on the wall behind the man.

"Mr West?" Hennessey asked.

"Yes."

"Inspector Hennessey, City of York police."

"Ah . . ."

"Are you a King's man? He nodded to the photograph."

"Gonville and Caius. It's just on the photograph, to the right of the chapel. A bit of it anyway."

"Yes, I know."

"Are you a Cambridge man?" West smiled.

"No, I'm a Trafalgar man."

"Sorry?"

"Trafalgar Road School, Greenwich, London. I left when I was fifteen. The building doesn't exist any more, it was pulled down to make room for a block of flats. My son attended Cambridge, though, Downing."

"Ah . . ."

"I've strolled the Backs with him. He's a barrister now. I catch 'em and he acquits them. Different cogs, same system."

"Yes. It makes you wonder how many people would be out of a job if other people didn't commit crime."

"Hundreds."

"Thousands, I'd say, to say nothing of all those dangerous crime writers who'd then have nothing to write about and would have to drive a bus for a living."

"Do them good." Hennessey settled in the chair, settling into West's company. "You must have enjoyed Cambridge. I mean, to have a photograph of part of the institution in your office."

"It does stimulate the pupils, transmits the message that such portals are accessible with a little application. But, yes, I did enjoy my years there."

"Charles, my son, didn't. He told me later, years after he had left."

"Oh?"

"He found the ex-public school ethos of the university overbearing. He found little acceptance and only then if he acknowledged his place as the token 'workie' in the college. He survived by taking lodgings in Romsey Town."

"Other side of the track."

"Literally. In the evenings he would go for a beer in one or the other of the working-class pubs in the city, where he felt more at home. But he survived, came home a lot more polished than he was when he went away. Now he's quite pukka, it's really rubbed off on him. By the way he carries himself now, you'd think he'd gone to Eton instead of a comprehensive school in the Vale of York. But he's pulled himself up a notch and educates his own children at fee-paying grammar schools."

"As our meritocracy allows."

"Indeed."

"I can understand his difficulty. I didn't at the time. I went to Taunton and felt quite at home at Cambridge but, since teaching in the public sector, I can fully understand just what formidable barriers are presented by the British class barriers."

"You've given your working life to public sector education?"

"Not as altruistic as it sounds, the service conditions in the public sector are excellent, the pension can't be bettered, the salary is very remunerative if you're high enough up the scale. The junior teachers with modest qualification, the timetable fodder, as they are known, scratch pennies, but with a few years' service, a move up the scale, a Head of Department and, yes, it's very attractive and also very rewarding."

"Enough to buy a home in France?"

West's eyes narrowed, a look of coldness shot across them. Hennessey saw then that West could become very unpleasant of personality and do so within a millisecond.

"You've been checking up on me, Inspector?"

"A question here and there."

"I make no secret of my holiday home. A two-bedroom cottage purchased in a run-down condition some years ago when such property was all but being given away. But you didn't come here to talk about illustrious universities or cottages in France?"

"No, I didn't. I came to ask for a bit of information."

"About?"

"Nathan Ossler."

West paled at the mention of Ossler's name. He recovered quickly, but the name clearly meant something to him.

"Do you know him, Mr West?" Hennessey pressed. He saw that the self-assured headmaster of just a few seconds ago was now uncomfortable in the extreme. Indeed, he seemed to Hennessey to be a very worried man. West paused, then said, "Yes. Yes, I do know him."

"In what capacity?"

"Is this about his murder? I read of it in the *Yorkshire Post* this morning."

"Yes, it is. How did you know him?"

"Fleetingly. Briefly."

"But well enough to phone him from here, at seven thirty on Friday evening last? Just over forty-eight hours before he was murdered?"

"How did you know that?"

"I didn't really, not until you said that."

West grimaced.

"So, how do you know him?"

"We met in a pub. I didn't like him. He latched on to me. A bit of a social climber, I thought. I phoned him on Friday to tell him that I couldn't go out for a beer with him this weekend. I have to make all the final preparations for our holiday in France. I said that I could possibly raise a glass with him in September. He's very pushy, doesn't take 'no' for an answer easily. I felt I had to offer him something. He's not a pleasant man."

"I see." Hennessey spoke softly, eyeing West, fixing him with a gimlet eye. "Where were you on Sunday evening between ten and midnight?"

"Sunday . . . ?"

"Two nights ago."

"I'm aware of that," West replied snappily, nervously.

"So, where were you?"

"I went to the Oak for a beer, last hour before closing on Sunday. As is my wont."

"The Oak?"

"A pub."

"So I gathered."

"In the village where I live. Little Scotterley."

"I don't know that village."

"North and east of York."

"Not too far from here then?"

"No. In fact some of our pupils live in the Scotterlies."

"How many Scotterlies are there?"

"Three. Great, Little and Middle Scotterly."

"I see. Who did you drink with?"

"Nobody. That is nobody in particular. Stood at the bar. Chatted to the publican."

"So, when did you last see Mr Ossler?"

"See him? Months ago. We didn't have a close contact."

"So you wouldn't know who would want to murder him?"

"No. But I can imagine someone wanting to do so. I won't be attending his funeral. I found him difficult to like."

"That's the impression I am getting of the man." Hennessey stood and noted a clear sign of relief on the part of West as he did so. "Not universally popular was our dear departed brother. When do you leave for France?"

"This coming Saturday. Why?"

"Never know when we'll have to speak to whom in an investigation like this, Mr West. Just never know. Good day."

Yellich would look back on a pleasant day's work, a very pleasant day's work indeed, the sort of day wherein the work was easy, but yet rattled the inquiry along nicely, very nicely indeed. It was also a day of surprises. He did, for example, find that a wooden shed can be described as a warehouse.

He left Micklegate Bar Police Station and drove to Tang Hall Estate to the house of Mrs Ossler's brother. Sadie Ossler answered the door. She looked to Yellich to be drawn, dishevelled, and sunken-eyed and he didn't doubt that, should she lift the sleeve of the black blouse she was wearing, she would reveal the telltale track marks of an intravenous drug habit. She blinked questioningly at Yellich, holding the door grudgingly ajar, in a posture which Yellich thought was defensive of her brother's tenancy. "I need to access your home, please," he explained.

"Why?"

"To obtain the key to the warehouse."

"Oh . . ." She turned disinterestedly into the gloom of the small council house and returned a few moments later with a bunch of house keys on a key ring, the fob of which was metal and enamel and said "Florida" in large yellow letters on a white background.

"Thanks." Yellich took the keys. "Where will I find the keys to the warehouse?"

"Try the desk drawer in his office . . . not the workroom where he was shot, but the other room, his den." She shut the door on him without further comment.

Yellich drove out to Strensall. He was not perturbed by Sadie Ossler's attitude, a young woman, bereaved, out of her depth by events which had overtaken her. He did hope for her sake that she wasn't turning to heroin to anaesthetise herself. If so, he thought, the fortune that she is likely to inherit will slip rapidly through her fingers. He reached Strensall after, he thought, too short a drive along a virtually, at that time of day, traffic-free road between flat green fields under a wide blue sky, and halted his car outside the newly built, inappropriately named Thundercliffe Grange. The blue and white police tape hung limply across the gateposts but the presence of a constable was no longer thought necessary. Yellich stepped over the tape and opened the gates, crunched a few feet along the gravel drive and then side-stepped on to the lawn and found it surprising that a path had not been worn across the lawn by a succession of folk avoiding the gravel, or at least along the side of the lawn if the direct route across the lawn might have been considered too great an act of trespass.

He let himself into the property. It was, he felt, eerily quiet. He moved quietly as if the house demanded a certain respect, and yet also there was an atmosphere about the building, as if the stress and conflict which had gone on within the walls had still remained somehow, even though the people had left either permanently, in the case of Nathan Ossler, or temporarily, in the case of his waiflike wife.

Yellich found the keys, two in all, just where Sadie Ossler had said they were likely to be, in a drawer in a desk of his office, conveniently labelled "warehouse" among a collection of other keys, some of which were labelled, some not. He retreated from the house. It was the only word he felt appropriate, retreat, to withdraw in good order, locked the premises behind him and drove to Haxby airfield, near Wetherby.

It was hard not to smile and so Yellich did so. So this, he thought, this is the warehouse, and wondered what lies Ossler had been telling his wife and hard-bitten secretary. For this was not in any man's language, a warehouse, this, in any man's language was a shed. It was neatly painted, it had a row of plants either side of the front door. It was at the address given, a disused airfield, now a business park, surrounded by modern buildings, each of which buzzed with shirt-sleeved or summer-skirted activity and it was the correct building, the sign on the front door OSSLER INCORPORATED said so. But a warehouse, it was not.

The interior was even less impressive than the exterior. Inside it was almost empty. A filing cabinet and a desk with a chair were the only items in the building. The remainder was merely walls and ceiling and floor of naked, untreated pine wood. Yellich left the door open, allowing the shed to "breathe" for he found the air stuffy and sour, caused by the summer conditions and the lack of ventilation. He crossed the echoing floor to the desk and the filing cabinet and found that the second key on the keyring, the smaller of the two, was the key to the filing cabinet. That too was empty, save for two loose-leaf files, one labelled West and the other labelled Hargrave. He sat at the desk and began to read.

The West file first. It was, of the two, simply the first that came to hand. It contained only a photocopy of an article which had clearly been printed twenty years earlier by the *Luton Chronicle* entitled "Local Hero". It showed the photograph of a beaming Nigel West "aged 20 years" which formed part of a story about a "locally born" Nigel, now a student at Derwent Teacher Training College in Carlisle, who had rescued a fellow student when the latter had "got into difficulty" while canoeing on Coniston Water and was in danger of drowning. Nigel West was quoted as saying, "It was nothing really, I was just there, I don't know what all the fuss is about." The article concluded that "Nigel hopes to qualify as a PE teacher in twelve months' time". And that was all the file contained and a bemused and perplexed Yellich said "So what?" to himself and laid the file on the desk top.

The file labelled Hargrave was equally sparse in terms of content. A copy of a marriage certificate of five years previous, one Richard Humby married Thomasina Hargrave at St Oswald's Church, Little Handy, West Yorkshire. The Hargrave file was not though sparse in terms of information, for it contained a second marriage certificate, this time of the marriage at York Registry Office dated three years earlier than the first marriage certificate, recording the marriage of Richard Humby and Claire Longstreet. This, Yellich thought, could only mean one thing, especially since George Hennessey had told him about Ossler describing himself as a professional blackmailer, "the trick is to turn the screw on people who can't go to the police". Yellich looked out of the window of the shed at a jet plane's white vapour trail high up in the blue and said "bigamy". He collected both files, and locking the door of the shed, being the premises of OSSLER INCORPORATED, behind him, carried them to his car and drove away.

Hennessey drove to the village of Little Scotterly and parked his car in the square, doubtless, he felt, it was the scene of a busy market at least one day per week, though at the time the polished cobbles served as a rare restriction-free car parking space. He had never been to the village before, as he had earlier indicated to Nigel West, and found it pleasing to the eye. The buildings on either side of the square seemed to converge on an ancient church with a square tower, an equally ancient yew in the boneyard and with a set of decaying stocks by the church gate, but not on sanctified ground itself. A war memorial stood at the further end of the square, which, by its shape, appeared to be a scaled-down version of Cleopatra's Needle. Hennessey walked towards it, it having lately become his habit to make a point of reading the names on each memorial which he had not previously encountered. He didn't know why he did it, an act of gratitude? An act of compassion for those who had died so young in a foreign land, and in a war that was not of their making and then only after enduring such hardships? And it was sparing a thought for the women: each name represented a young widow who would face a bleak future, or a woman who would never find a husband. Perhaps, he thought, it was a gesture of thanks for his own now gentle and silvered existence. Or perhaps it was because his own elder brother had failed to make it through the "danger years" by reason of motorcycle rather than enemy action, and following his death there had always been a hole in Hennessey's life where there should have been someone to follow.

The village of Little Scotterly, he found, had given fifteen sons to "the War to end all wars", three with the surname Toose and a fourth with the surname Tooze. He hoped the mason had not made a mistake; surely not another Toose? The 1939–1945 war had claimed three more village boys though none had a surname that also appeared on the 1914–1918 column of war dead. In Little Scotterly, in the first half of the twentieth century, if you gave a son to the First War, you didn't give a son to the second, or vice versa.

He turned and surveyed the village; white painted buildings, half-timbered, old sunken roofs. It had, Hennessey thought, an earlier era quality about it. The shops had sun awnings pulled out of the wall above their windows which shaded goods laid out on the pavement for inspection prior to purchase. The pace of the village seemed slower somehow, the speed of the pedestrians, and of the tractor driven through the village by a blonde, bronzed, bare-chested youth, who clearly lived in more fortunate times – not for him an early death in a foreign field by the hand of a man who didn't know his name.

Hennessey found the Oak. He found it very easily. It was

the source of the only bustle in the centre of Little Scotterly. A skip stood in the road outside it, a funnel of yellow plastic buckets, suspended from the roof of the pub led to the skip and occasionally masonry and plaster were tipped down the tunnel and rattled in a dust cloud in the skip. Men in heavy boots, and jeans, open-shirted, some bare-chested, laboured about the building. Hennessey approached, and even from the pavement, became aware of the sound of power drills and the heavy, sickly sweet smell of solvent vapour coming from within the building. A man in a blue hard-hat stood outside the pub and seemed, to Hennessey, to have, by the way he carried himself, some supervisory capacity. He approached the man. "Busy?" he asked.

"Couldn't be busier." The man had a pleasant, affable manner so Hennessey found. "But we're on time."

"Good for you. On time?"

"We're refitting and refurbishing and renewing the roof. First refurbishing for thirty years. Started three weeks ago, one week to go. But we're on time."

"Been closed for three weeks, you say?"

"Aye. Grand reopening in a week's time, free drink for the crew that day if we maintain the schedule. But we'll do it. This is a good crew, solid grafters, each one, bunch of good lads, set 'em to a task and leave 'em at it. Don't get many crews like this one."

"Lucky you. Is there another pub in the village?"

"The Viscount Keppel, yonder." The man pointed along the road. "See the sign?"

"Ah, yes."

"It's been the only pub in the village for the last three weeks, it's been doing great business."

"I'll bet it has. Thanks." Hennessey stepped on the road

side of the skip and walked towards The Viscount Keppel. It was, he thought, curious, or perhaps it was not so curious. If Nigel West, Headmaster of Crosshill School had in fact done the very un-Headmasterly thing and gone for a drink in a pub on Sunday evening last, he had not, as he had claimed, gone to the Oak. That was very clear.

The entrance to The Viscount Keppel was via a narrow door and a cool and a narrow panelled corridor which led to a long narrow bar. Hennessey halted just inside the entrance to the pub to read a framed note about the venerated person after whom the public house was named. "Augustus Keppel," it read "second son of the Earl of Albemarle, born twenty-fifth of April 1725, served under Hawke in 1757, captured Gorée in 1758, took part in the battle of Quiberon Bay in 1759 and commanded at the capture of Havana in 1762. In 1778 he encountered the French fleet off Ushant on twenty-seventh of July, but owing to a disagreement between Keppel and Palliser, his second in command, the French were suffered to escape. Both admirals were tried by court martial but acquitted. In 1782 he was created Viscount Keppel and became the First Lord of the Admiralty. He died in 1786."

"Well," Hennessey said to himself. "One lives and one learns." He walked to the end of a corridor, turned into the bar and nodded to the publican a man of, Hennessey thought, false good humour; instantly friendly. Such people Hennessey had found have very low flash points and can turn very unpleasant in an instant. "Just reading about Viscount Keppel. I'd heard the name but I had thought that he was executed."

"You're thinking of Byng." The false, jolly publican wiped a pint glass with a towel. "Same era, but he's the

Johnny that lost Minorca to the French, so they shot him. A lot of people get them confused. There's a column to Keppel in Rotherham, a sort of north country Nelson's column but the regulars in here are divided as to which Keppel the column was erected in memory of. There was an Admiral Keppel in the nineteenth century. Both Keppels were admirals but only one was a viscount. The pub is definitely named after the Viscount but nobody can be bothered to travel to Rotherham to research the column."

"I see."

"What would you like to drink, sir?"

"Nothing."

And George Hennessey was neither disappointed nor surprised to see the joviality of the publican change rapidly to a scowl.

"Police," he said.

"Oh . . ." and the joviality returned.

"I'd like a little information about a gentleman called West, he lives in the village and drinks locally, so he tells me."

"Nigel West, the headmaster of the school over at . . ."

"Crosshill Comprehensive, yes, that's he."

"Bit of a toff, approachable though, white house at the end of the village, past the church. It used to be the rectory, and it reckons to be haunted. I mean what would a rectory be without a ghost?"

"What indeed."

"But he's not really a drinking man, not a pub goer anyway." The publican replaced the glass and wiped the polished wooden bar top.

"Interesting."

"That's not for me to say really, but if Mr West tipples

at all, he tipples at home. I mean this village forms part of the catchment area of his school, many of his pupils come in here or the Oak for a drink and we have to chuck 'em out but they're flyer than a barrel load of monkeys, particularly the girls, they can dress up and pass for nineteen-year-olds, when they're only fourteen or fifteen. Then we get prosecuted for selling alcohol to children, and all the magistrates see is a fourteen-year-old girl in her school uniform looking sheepish and the beaks think that's how she looked when she was served her vodka and tonic. Makes us look bad."

"Occupational hazard, I'd say."

"It's more than a hazard if your livelihood's on the line." It was a sharp, ill-tempered retort and Hennessey wondered if the Viscount Keppel was known for trouble. He had once read a study into pub violence which concluded that along with factors like the social area in which the pub is situated, the attitude of the publican is critical. An over-controlling publican who fails to realise that it is the patrons, not he, who control the pub, can lead to resentment and hence violence among customers.

"But Mr West didn't come in here?"

"I know him and I've never seen him in here."

"The Oak then? Would you know?"

"I've never heard tell of him go in there. It attracts the younger set, and he's more likely to rub shoulders with his pupils in there than in here. Of the two pubs in the village, he's likely to come in here and like I said, I've never seen him."

"Well, thanks. The white house at the end of the village, you say?"

"Past the church, you can't miss it. It's called the Old

Rectory. Yews either side of the drive, metal railings round the garden."

Hennessey found the building easily, being where the publican of the Viscount said it would be and with the appearance he had described. He walked up the driveway, an alert springer spaniel announcing his arrival. He stopped short of the door, staying reverently at the foot of the steps knowing that the dog's frantic barking would force a response from within the house. It came in the form of a small, finely made, nervous-looking woman who did not, to Hennessey's mind, fit the mould of the headmaster's wife. The woman seemed to have "guilty" written on her forehead, so thought Hennessey, and he also saw fear in her eyes.

"He's not here," she said quickly, apologetically.

"Who?"

"My husband. He's not here."

"How do you know it's him that I have come to see?"

"Well who else would anybody come to see? Who are you anyway?"

"Police." He showed his ID. "Nothing to be alarmed about."

"Oh . . . what . . . is it one of the children?"

"No . . . no . . . I told you, Mrs West, it's nothing to be alarmed about." Hennessey took off his hat and felt the sun on his thinned hair and scalp. He found time to enjoy the blackbird's song and his eye was caught by a grey squirrel scurrying up a tree beside the West's house. He replaced his hat. He knew from experience that the scalp is no place to be sunburned.

"My husband's at work."

"I know, I've just visited him."

"Oh . . . why . . . ?"

"Where were you on Sunday evening, Mrs West?"

"Here. All evening. Just me and the children. All evening, yes, all evening. Why?"

"Your husband wasn't home with you?"

"No. He went out."

"Where?"

"He didn't tell me . . . he never does. He says it's not my place to know."

"He says that?"

"Don't all men? And he makes the decisions. I've got to pack. We're going to France you see, on holiday. My husband owns a house there."

"He owns it? *He*?"

"Yes. He owns it. I've got to go. It's supposed to be done by the time he gets home . . . he's got a terrible temper. If anything isn't right . . ."

"Wait a moment," Hennessey insisted, allowing a note of authority to enter his voice.

"Yes?" But by now the door was half closed, a fearful, thin face peered between the door and the frame.

"What time did your husband go out on Sunday evening?"

"About nine o'clock."

"And return?"

"After midnight."

"Was there beer on his breath?"

"No . . . no. My husband doesn't drink." She shut the door firmly and Hennessey heard her running into the old rambling building, hurrying to do the packing, to do it perfectly before He gets home.

Like father, like son. Yellich, never having met Nathan Ossler, thought that he could well imagine him in life if the adage about fathers and sons was accurate. For here was Oliver Ossler, a thin, and thin-faced man, a sharp dresser, gold-capped teeth, who smiled because it seemed to Yellich that he muchly liked himself, though Yellich did not like him at all, right from the outset.

"Me and his wife," sneered Ossler. "Me and that mousy thing from the children's home and the gutter. The will has yet to be read but me, me and thing, we have been advised by my father that his will is clear, she gets the house and all the contents, lock, stock and barrel, all bought and paid for, I get his capital. My father had his faults but he did what he said he'd do: always. Always did something if he said he was going to do it. Sometimes did something without saying he was going to do it, but he never said he'd do something and then not do it. So we already know how much she's worth, a-lot-of-money. She won't be able to afford to continue living there but if she plays her cards right – sells it, trades down – she won't have any money troubles for the rest of her natural. Me, I'm left with either a few pounds or a few million pounds or anything in between depending on how much daddy dearest had in his Post Office savings account. Thundercliffe Grange . . . would you credit it. I remember watching television when I was about ten years old, dad was in the room, we were watching a TV drama, some costume drama or other and a house was called 'Thundercliffe Grange' and dad said, 'That's a good name for a house. I'll have that name for a house some day'."

"Does what he says, as you say." Yellich read the office, neat, controlled, dominated, small windows beneath a low medieval ceiling looked out onto the narrow bustle of Bootham Bar. A calendar behind the man revealed June to be a scantily dressed young female reclining over the bonnet of a black Porsche. He said "You're a businessman yourself?"

"Following the old man's footsteps, you mean? Well yes and no. Yes, in the sense that I am also like he was, a self-employed businessman, but no in the sense that I am not following in his shoes. I'm building my own business and doing well. I'm a factoring agent. I lend money to struggling companies against their assets. I lend when and where banks wouldn't in which case I can demand a high rate of interest, and I lend when and where banks would also lend but at a lower rate of interest. It's risk free really, as is the nature of usury. If they don't pay up, plus interest, I seize their assets. It's not a popular way of doing business."

"That I can well understand." Yellich inclined his head away from the man, she, the girl on the Porsche, had suddenly became a lot more attractive than Oliver Ossler and in a sense no less two-dimensional.

"But I have no shortage of customers. I have paid off my mortgage, own a Range Rover, and a yacht I keep at Hull Marina and I'm still nearer thirty than forty."

"Lucky you."

"Hard-working me, there is graft about this, it isn't a question of shaking the tree to make the golden apples fall, but it's better than working. Dad loaned me the money to get started. I took it from there. So no, I do not have a motive for murdering my father. Even if I do stand to inherit the balance of his bank account, plus any other liquid assets he may have."

Yellich raised his eyebrows.

"I watch detective stories on TV. Never read them of course, but I love a good murder mystery on the box, a bottle of wine, a bit of female company, so I've gotten to know that anyone who is involved or connected with the deceased in any way is automatically 'in the frame'. Is that the expression?"

"Yes, yes it is. But I've called to see you to request information as much as to eliminate you."

"Information?"

"We have found out that your mother was murdered a few years ago. Shot, just as your father was."

"Oh . . ." Oliver Ossler grimaced. "Yes. I was close to my mother." But the sudden show of emotion rapidly vanished.

"The similarity is obvious, we can't ignore the possibility that the two murders are connected despite the time gap."

"I can understand that but you'll know that mother had put on father's duffle-coat just to nip out to buy something, she and dad were the same build, the hood was up . . . it must have been a case of mistaken identity. I think you're looking at coincidence, not connection."

"Possibly. So you wouldn't know of anybody who'd want to murder your father?"

"It's probably. Probably the murders of both my parents by the same manner is coincidence. But the answer to the question is no. No, I don't know of anyone who would want to murder my father. He was a businessman. Businessmen make enemies. The more successful you are, the more enemies you make. It comes with the territory."

"What exactly was your father's line of business?"

"Now you're asking. You've put your finger on something odd, something that I could never fathom."

"Oh?"

"Well, he advanced me money to get started. I paid him back with interest, most businessmen want their sons to take

100

over their business, but dad just said 'too many fingers in too many pies', said it was best for me to start fresh, so there was capital to get me going, there was advice, encouragement, but nothing to take over."

"I see. You do have an alibi for Sunday evening?"

"Yes. I was away for the weekend. I have a new lady friend, she . . . well, we have just taken up with each other and she wanted to go away to start . . . to consummate our relationship. So we went to a hotel in Derbyshire, to the Peak District, got back to York late Sunday evening and having got off the ground as it were, I spent the remainder of Sunday/Monday night in her flat. I came to work on Monday, yesterday, and a constable came to the office to break the news. If I don't seem distraught it's my way of coping. I can't go to his house because it's not mine to inherit, and I was asked to refrain from entering it . . . what did the constable say? It's a 'crime scene'. So I've come to work to do something, better than moping at home. And no, I don't posses a gun. Besides which, I have no motive. Like I've just said, I may even be wealthier than my father, depending . . . well, we'll see what we shall see. I also don't think I'm capable of it."

"It?"

"Murder. The pulling of a trigger, the plunging of a knife. The most serious of all offences, it's the speediest to perpetrate, requires no apprenticeship in the criminal fraternity, little skill or strength. Most people have fantasised about doing it at some point, but so few do and I don't think it's the consequences that prevent folk from murdering someone, I think there's an immense psychological barrier to the act of deliberate taking of life. I couldn't get over that barrier, especially with respect to my old man."

"I'm relieved to hear it."

"No, your perpetrator is going to have a heart made out of granite. Me, I don't think I ever would give into that impulse, you know, the best revenge a man or woman can ever take."

"Tell me."

"Let yourself be seen to be enjoying life. Your enemies can't handle it. They just can't handle it."

"She's out riding." The man had a bristlingly immaculate appearance: brown jacket, yellow waistcoat which surprisingly, to Hennessey's eyes, didn't clash; plus-fours, thick socks, even in this weather; brogues, pencil-thin moustache, smelled of aftershave and pipe tobacco. "How did you find us, anyway?"

"Golf club secretary. And it's really you I want to see."

"He shouldn't be so free with that sort of information. Members' addresses, indeed."

"He wasn't free with it. He was very reluctant to part with it, in fairness to him. I told him it was in connection with a murder inquiry and advised him I could obtain a warrant if necessary."

"Better." The man stepped back from the threshold of his house. "Come in, please, Chief Inspector."

Inside the large house was cool which Hennessey felt explained the man's woollen clothing. It smelled of furniture polish and was well stocked with potted plants. Hennessey was invited to the drawing-room, Hargraves stood in front of the fire, hands behind his back. Behind him on the mantelpiece was a framed photograph of a man in an army officer's uniform and a woman in a long tartan skirt standing outside the registry office in Gretna Green.

The lady was taller than the man and younger. A lot younger.

"You're an army man?" Hennessey observed.

"Was . . . was in the Regular Army. Yorks and Lancs . . . infantry . . . I didn't make staff college, retired as a major . . . have a pension and I run the local cadet corps."

"I see."

"Pay is modest in the extreme."

"Really. You could have fooled me." Hennessey allowed his approving look of the house to be seen. "It's not often that a police officer enters a house like this, not on duty anyway."

"My wife's family, they're moneyed."

"I see."

"I provided the genes." He said suddenly before Hennessey could move the conversation.

"I'm sorry?"

"They have money and background. I only have background, but that's important, don't you know?"

"No, I didn't know, but I'll take your word for it."

"It is." The man sniffed smugly.

"You'll have heard of the murder of Nathan Ossler?"

"I have. Can't say that I'm sorry. Can't say I'm sorry at all."

"Oh?"

"I believe that a more unpleasant man has not walked on the earth since Genghis Khan."

"Yes . . . I can understand your emotion. I have heard about the altercation at the Golf Club."

"Poured beer down my wife's front," said with controlled anger. "And I don't mean down the outside front of her dress, I mean down her front . . ."

"I get the picture. It'd make any man angry."

"Made me furious. And I don't mean furious. I mean furious. It's all very well for him. At least it was all very well for him being self-employed, he hasn't got a position to lose. I could lose my commission for criminal activity, well, for a conviction of a criminal act. But I controlled myself. He was expelled from the Golf Club and that hurt him, being a social climber, as he was. But money doesn't open every door, that's where background comes in and that's what irked him. I haven't anything like the income he could generate, but I can go places he couldn't go."

"So you were not furious enough to kill him?"

Hargrave flushed, a look of anger shot across his eyes. Hennessey saw it and here he saw a man who could kill. "That's not even remotely funny, Inspector."

"I'll say it's not, in fact it's very close at hand in its seriousness. Hence my interest. So, you're not at work today?"

"The cadet corps doesn't take up all my time. I'll be there this evening, every Tuesday evening, some drill, some unarmed combat, so I have time off in lieu during the day."

"So where were you on Sunday evening last, after ten p.m.?"

A pause. "Why? Am I under suspicion?"

"You have a motive. I've known men murder for less, I mean honour is quite important, is it not? I mean among people with . . . er . . . background?"

"Yes. Yes it is . . . but affront to my honour and my wife's honour is not sufficient to make me turn criminal. Have to retain occupancy of the moral high ground, you see. Besides, he was blackballed from the Golf Club. That was enough for me and Lucille."

"Lucille being your wife?"

"Yes. Lucille Hargrave, of the Scarborough Hargraves. You'll know the family."

"I confess I don't."

"Mm. Fishing and agriculture in the main. That sort of thing."

"The Squirearchy?"

"In a word."

"So you are Major Hargrave?"

"I am."

"You took your wife's name upon marriage?"

"As you see. It's only convention that a woman takes her husband's name. It's not the law."

"I never knew that. But anyway, back to the question of your whereabouts on Sunday evening."

"Here."

"Alone?"

"Yes."

"All evening?"

"From six p.m. until midnight, or a little after. Half past midnight maybe. My wife was out with her girlfriends."

"So you have no alibi for the time of Nathan Ossler's murder?"

"If that's when he was murdered, no I haven't."

"And you have a motive, despite what you say."

"I dare say I do. I'm not sorry he's no longer with us."

"Do you own a gun, Major?"

"A couple of shotguns."

"A handgun?"

"No."

"Plenty of access to them, though?"

"A whole armoury."

105

"What are the calibre of the guns?"

"The handguns are .22. We use them for target practice."

"That's interesting."

"Why, was he shot with a .22?"

"Probably. Would you know how to make a dumdum bullet."

"Yes. Every soldier learns that one. You take a sharp knife and cut a cross on the head of the bullet. It makes the bullet explode on impact with its target. They make a right mess of a human being."

"Well, thanks, Major Hargrave. Just called to check a few things. It may be that we'll call back."

"We?"

"The police."

Leaving Oliver Ossler's cramped office space, Yellich walked back through the city centre, picked up his car from the car park at Micklegate Bar Police Station and drove out to Strensall. He criss-crossed the village until he was satisfied that, not at all to his surprise, it didn't contain an Indian restaurant and then began to drive slowly back towards York. While on Malton Road entering Heworth, he saw a restaurant called "Fariq's", small, modest in appearance, but definitely Indian. He parked his car and walked up to it. It was shut. He knocked on the door anyway. It was opened rapidly. A young Asian man held the door wide and said in a solid Yorkshire accent, "We're closed, mate."

"'S all right, mate." Yellich showed his ID. "I'm not hungry, yet."

The manager, Mr Fariq himself, was middle-aged and overweight and his office was, Yellich thought, even more cramped than was Oliver Ossler's office. Mr Fariq, though, was very helpful and searched his invoices of the work done the previous Sunday. He found the receipt for the delivery to "Ozzler", Thun/cliffe Grange, Strensall, timed as ten thirty p.m.

"That's when he phoned it in," said Mr Fariq, who spoke with an Asian accent, but was, Yellich found, word perfect with his English. "Allowing time to prepare it and deliver it, he would have received it by about eleven fifteen that evening."

"Eleven fifteen approx.," said Yellich as he wrote the time in his notebook.

"Briefly," Hennessey said, "just make it brief, the nuts and bolts. I want us to sleep on this more than address it." He sat forwards, leaning his elbows on his desk top and ran his mottled hands and fingers through his silver hair.

"Well, briefly." Yellich sat in the chair in front of Hennessey's desk, his lightweight summer jacket folded across his knees. He consulted his notebook. "Dr D'Acre was right about the meal, it was Indian. I found the restaurant, it confirms a delivery of a meal late on Sunday which would narrow the time of death down nicely. They reckon a delivery time of about eleven fifteen p.m. He ate the meal, there was no unfinished meal at the crime scene. That would put the time of death close to midnight. Narrows it down, like I said. Had no luck with Oliver Ossler, a bit hard bitten but clean as a new pin regarding his father's murder. Had some luck at the warehouse which is a large wooden hut." He dropped two files on Hennessey's desk. "I brought these for you to read, one's clear, the Hargrave file, as clear a case of bigamy as I have seen. So I would assume."

Hennessey opened the Hargrave file. He held the copies of the two marriage certificates. In the absence of a death certificate in respect of wife number one, or a decree nisi, it would make Hargrave or Humby a bigamist.

"It would make him a bigamist." Hennessey leaned back in his chair. "I've just visited him, he's very well set up but makes no bones about it being his wife's family's money. He married for money, big mistake. It's a useful adage you know, Sergeant, 'go where money is, but never marry for it'."

"But he married for it?"

"Makes no bones about it, as I said. Puts him well in the frame, a definite revisit."

"Did he have an alibi?"

"No, just said he was home alone all evening." Hennessey sighed. "Pity that. No alibi. Give me an alibi merchant each time, every time, it's the ones that know the value of leaving the burden of proof with the police that annoy me, especially since they're invariably as guilty as sin itself."

"In the frame you say, boss?"

"Ossler was a blackmailer, remember, he boasted to the Scoutmaster that he was a professional blackmailer, the trick being . . . what was it he said? The trick being that you can't put the screws on people who can go to the police. He read the Scoutmaster wrong and collected a term as a guest of Her Majesty. He clearly was disinclined to repeat that mistake and what a lovely victim Major Hargrave makes. One word to his wife and he's cut off without a penny and will lose his job in the cadet force. Station in life is very important to the good major. He made that plain, and Ossler had him by the short and curlies. He's probably been milking him for years, got greedy, made Hargrave ponder dangerous thoughts about the cadet force's armoury and the .22 target pistols it contains. He knows how to make a dumdum bullet, as any soldier does in fairness, but he also knows a fragmenting bullet can't be matched to the barrel of a specific gun. It would be a very easy matter to 'borrow' a gun from the armoury and a few rounds of ammunition."

"Solemn," said Yellich. "Solemn, very, very solemn."

"A definite revisit."

"The other file doesn't mean much in itself, at least not so far as I can see."

"Tell me about it."

"It's about a fella called West. It's a photocopy of an article that appeared in a Bedford newspaper, entitled 'Local Hero'. The article's about twenty years old. Apparently, a local lad called West saved another youngster from drowning in a lake in the Lake District when they were both students at a college for trainee gym teachers in Carlisle. So, if the fella West is still alive, he'll be a fortysomething gym teacher now."

"Well he's alive all right," Hennessey took the file from Yellich, "except he's not a gym teacher, he's a youthful headmaster of a large comprehensive school and he isn't of humble origins in Bedford, he went to Taunton Public School and the University of Cambridge. Or so he'd have you believe."

"Well, solemn . . . oh, so solemn. Another lovely target for blackmail, another poor guy who can't go to the law."

"Less of the 'poor guy', Yellich. If he didn't go to Cambridge University, every salary cheque he has received from the local authority has been an act of obtaining money by false pretences."

"How on earth can you do it, boss? You can't fabricate

qualifications and you'll need references from your university to get a job."

"That we'll probably find out, Yellich. But here we have two people with a very strong motive to murder Nathan Ossler and, if nothing else, we have two felons who'll help improve our clear-up rate. And that is it for today. We've both got homes to go to."

Yellich returned home to his modest modern semi-detached house in Huntingdon. He kissed his wife and went to the front room to seek his son, whom he knew had been tiring his wife all day, though unintentionally. As often happened, as soon as he was home his wife went upstairs to lie down for an hour. His son, slender, like his parents, looked smart in his short trousers and shiny shoes and bow tie, like many twelve-year-olds. He kissed Yellich and held his arm and said "time?"

"All right." Yellich sat on the settee and his son went to the corner of the room, stepping over scattered toys as he did so and picked up a model clock with moveable hands. He returned to the settee and sat next to Yellich. He held the toy clock on his lap and looked eagerly at his father who said, "Three o'clock" and the twelve-year-old moved the hands to the three o'clock position. Yellich hugged him and said "Good boy . . . seven o'clock." And so the game progressed for half an hour with Yellich requesting increasingly complicated times, "twenty-three minutes past nine . . . six forty-five . . .", doing really what the medical people had asked of him and his wife. With stimulation and love and encouragement, they had said, Sam should be able to function as a twelve-year-old by the time he is twenty or twenty-five when he'll be able to live at least semi

110

independently. A place in a hostel, his own room, access to a kitchen for self-catered snacks, but with staff on hand to supervise, to prepare the main meals and so forth. Yellich found that he enjoyed his parenting. His son's condition had been like a new world opening up to him and he and his wife had made very good friends of people whose children also had learning difficulties. And the magical years had been prolonged. While parents of other twelve-year-olds had begun to experience problems with their child's behaviour, he and his wife had enjoyed the magical, endlessly trusting period which for them had seemed to continue far longer than the allotted four or five years. Yet there was also a gnawing sadness, a guilt, which had increased and decreased but was always there. Heightened especially when he realised his wife had been hanging on until he came home so that she could go upstairs and collapse on her bed for an hour. But that Sam was not at all distressed when he returned, meant that Hilary had not given in to ill-tempered frustration. And if she had ever done so he could understand because being with a twelve-year-old three-year-old all day is not easy, not easy at all. For, as his father had once said to her "men in war get medals for less". But she just never had given in, and mainly because of her, not him, Sam was well on his way to semi-independent living, that Yellich knew and knew well.

First it had been Graham and his beloved Norton. Then it had been Jennifer. But both mercifully had known little if anything.

George Hennessey sat on the chair on the patio of the rear of his house in Easingwold. He had returned home and let himself in the large four-bedroom detached house on Thirsk Road to be greeted by a tail wagging, barking with joy – Oscar, his brown mongrel, and "best pal".

He had taken Oscar for a walk and had then returned, whereupon he prepared meals for both he and Oscar. He had then been lured out to the rear of the house by a scarlet sunset, which seemed to cover the entire north western quadrant of the sky. Though lure, he thought, was not quite the right word because each day, no matter what the season, no matter what the weather, if he was at home and not laid up ill, he had always gone into the rear garden and said "hello" to Jennifer whom no woman, he felt, could replace.

The house had been their first mortgage, they had been mortgaged up to the hilt, really beyond their means, but they had moved in and been oh so deliriously happy and content and fulfilled. But their garden, Jennifer had felt, had been dull, just a small square lawn to the front of the house and a large, nay vast, flat lawn to the rear. And so Jennifer, whom Hennessey recalled, knew only how to grow and nurture living things, had, when she was heavily pregnant with their first child, sat down one day, pen and paper in hand and had re-designed their garden.

The front lawn needed to be bordered by a low privet she thought, and the rear lawn had to be divided widthways at the middle by a high privet with a gate set in the middle of the it. The final ten feet of the garden had to be left as waste land but with a pond dug for natural amphibia to colonise. Trees, too, would have to be planted to break up the flat skyline of the Vale within which the house and neighbouring houses seemed to be lost. She had once read that settlers on the prairies of the United States would plant trees so as to break up the monotony of the landscape and had said to a young George Hennessey, "that I can understand". And that year, Hennessey had been set to planting privet and building gates, and digging a pond in the part of the garden Jennifer referred to as "the going forth", having read Bacon's essay, "Of Gardens". Though their garden had been, and still was, less than Bacon's requisite minimum of thirty acres, it was still large enough to keep Hennessey trim and muscular.

Then, just when all was going well, all was going swimmingly, all could not be improved – it was he and her and by then Charles, three months old – Jennifer had died. She had been walking in the centre of Easingwold, carrying shopping bags on a hot day when her legs, it was reported, just seemed to buckle. Suspecting an incident of fainting, folk had gone to her aid, quickly, eager to help without a sense of a tragedy unfolding, but there was no pulse to be found. She was pronounced dead on arrival at York City Hospital and the inquest concurred with the medical diagnosis of Sudden Death Syndrome, which Hennessey felt said more about medical ignorance than it said about medical knowledge, like "ague" which become known as "malaria", eventually. And so, he felt that until medical knowledge advanced to the point that the medics could explain why life should suddenly, and without warning, leave a young person in the prime of life and in the fullest of health, humanity just had to live with Sudden Death Syndrome.

Her ashes were scattered on her beloved garden and each day, in whatever weather, if he was at home, he went into the garden and said "hello" to her. Sometimes he was there but briefly, sometimes, when troubled, he spoke to her at length. Latterly he had spent some time in the garden telling her about Louise, telling her that his feelings for had not diminished at all, not at all, that he had cherished her

113

memory in the intervening thirty years, and still cherished it, but that both Louise and he needed companionship of a romantic nature, that Louise's children had accepted and welcomed him, that Louise knew about her. All of that he explained and hoped that she understood. And when he had told the garden about Louise he had felt a sudden rush of warmth and a strong and very benevolent presence as of someone who wanted only to nurture living things.

Both had been young. Graham had been just twenty-two years old, and Hennessey recalled laying in bed listening to his older brother start up his motorcycle and roar away on it. Lying there, straining his ears to catch every last fading decibel as Graham had driven down Trafalgar Road towards the Maritime Museum and the Naval College, until finally the sound was swallowed by the sound of other traffic and ships' foghorns and a drunk with an Irish accent walking up Colomb Street beneath his window chanting his "Hail Mary's" very, very loudly. And later that same night a knock at the door, murmured voices and his mother's wailing and his father fighting back the tears as he told him that Graham had ridden his motorcycle to heaven because he wanted to get there ahead of us to save a place for us.

Then just twenty years later a uniformed officer had knocked on his door looking solemn and awkward and he knew then how his parents had felt, or perhaps he didn't, perhaps losing a partner can never be like losing a child, despite the emotion involved.

Jennifer had been twenty-three, one year of life more than Graham had had, and both had died in the summer. That had always seemed wrong somehow, he felt it was, well, just wrong, for a reason that he couldn't put his finger on. He had attended funerals and he had attended weddings and it had been his long-held observance that just as summer adds to a wedding, so winter adds to a funeral; the Minister saying "ashes to ashes" amid a snow flurry at his father's funeral had seemed so perfect. Yet Graham had been laid to rest amid lush grass, blue skies, and fluttering butterflies. It hadn't seemed right, it hadn't seemed right at all. It had been a day for Graham to take him for a spin on the Norton, a day for he and Jen to walk in the woods, arms round each other. Not a day for them to be put in a hole in the ground, or scattered, twenty years apart, but both had managed to leave a larger hole behind them than the hole they had filled, or could have filled, when they died and that, he felt, was how any person is measured upon their death. It's not the size of the hole they fill, it's the size of the hole they leave behind them. And there were other similarities, both the deaths had been so untimely that clerics had talked about "testing your faith" and "bringing you closer to God", they had both been those sorts of death.

George Hennessey sat on the patio looking at the garden under a red sky. First there had been Graham and then there had been Jennifer. The evening began to grow cool and so he decided to go inside and read more about the Napoleonic war for an hour or two, or until he felt ready for his bed and a good, nourishing sleep. Hennessey stood and smiled at the lawn, and the trees, and the privet, and the pond "going forth" and said "Goodnight, Jennifer, goodnight."

Five

In which Hennessey visits two women who are married and are not married, and the gracious reader learns more of the Chief Inspector's private life.

Hennessey thought it totally unnecessary for him to stand in front of the commander's desk, but the commander liked it that way and so he, the commander, got what he wanted. "Dapper", thought Hennessey, was the word that the great majority of people would use to describe Commander Sharkey. He was small for a police officer, dark suit, pencil-line moustache, piercing blue eyes. He had come to York City Police via a commission in the British Army and a period in the Royal Hong Kong Police, framed photographs of men in uniform on the wall behind him said so. He was a man, younger than Hennessey, who believed that there was a place for everything and that everything must remain in its place. And that included George Hennessey who stood, as expected, dead centre in front of the commander's desk. It was the Wednesday morning, the beginning of the third full working day of the inquiry and Commander Sharkey required "apprising".

"It seems the deceased was a blackmailer, sir." Hennessey

116

spoke calmly, comforted by his cynicism about the Commander's "game", as he saw it. "Not a pleasant fellow, one earlier attempt on his life resulted in the death of his first wife some eight years ago. It was probably prompted by that that he sold his house, which was within the walls apparently, and bought, or rather built, out at Strensall."

"A nice village."

"Yes, it is," Hennessey replied. "We're getting to know the place.

"Anyway, the deceased moved out there and was very security conscious: gravel drive, dogs, good expanse of lawn between the road and the house, rose bushes, high fencing, a frightened man or so it would seem."

"If he's blackmailing people he would be. You know if you're being blackmailed about something and you can't go to the police, there's only one of two things you can do, which is either pay up or bump the fellow off."

"Agreed, and in fact Ossler had learned his lesson about making sure that his victim couldn't go to the police. He apparently turned the screws on a Scoutmaster once but he'd misinterpreted some photographs. Apparently, the Scoutmaster and his boys went skinny dipping one very hot summer but it was nothing more than that. Ossler clearly saw it as evidence of paedophile activity. The Scoutmaster went to the police and Ossler collected five years, served three."

"And came out having learned a valuable lesson about the blackmail trade." Sharkey sniffed and glanced out of his window: tourists walking medieval walls beneath a cloudless blue sky.

"Clearly, sir. Also he probably learned not to ask for more than the victim could afford. The Scoutmaster told me that

117

if Ossler had asked for an affordable sum, he might have paid it."

"Understandable, even if it would have been a mistake."

"As you say, sir."

"So, despite the security measures, someone shot Ossler in his own home. Someone who could get past the dogs. That might narrow the field considerably."

"It might, sir, but it's best not to be blinkered about things. You can get past dogs if you spend time getting to know them and Ossler let his dogs have the run of the garden, so I'm keeping an open mind about that one. The people who the dogs knew – the present Mrs Ossler, the cleaning lady, who found the body, and the secretary – all have cast-iron alibis for the Sunday evening after eleven thirty p.m. We've been able to narrow the time of death down to a two-hour time window."

"I see. Other suspects?"

"Two, sir. Two men whom Ossler had information about, one of whom appears to be a bigamist and the other appears to have a very good job on the basis of a degree he doesn't possess. Neither of whom can go to the police and one of whom has access to firearms."

"Two days and some good progress already."

"I'd like to think so, sir. If nothing else, we've caught a bigamist and someone who's been obtaining money by deception. Help our clear-up rate if nothing else, as I said to Sergeant Yellich."

"Good. You'll keep me informed?"

"Of course."

Sharkey leaned to one side and opened a drawer in his desk. "I brought this for you to have a look at." He handed Hennessey a book. "I was rummaging through my boxes the other day and came across it. An out-of-print, a very out-of-print eye-witness account of the battle of Gettysburg from the Confederate point of view."

"Well . . ." Hennessey gripped the book. "Thank you."

"It's a loan, of course."

"Oh, of course, of course."

"The author claims to have survived Pickett's charge . . . as you'll read. But I chanced upon it and knew your interest in military history. I thought it would be well up your street."

"Thank you indeed, sir. I'll read it with interest. I'm back at Waterloo at the moment, a French account, in translation, but I'll put it on one side for this . . ."

"About a week? All right?"

"Be long enough, sir."

Hennessey walked down the corridor clutching the dusty, slim volume and returned to his office. The sudden and totally unexpected display of warmth from the usually ice-cold Commander had touched him deeply.

"It was his idea. And it seemed like a good idea at the time. It still does really. I heard he'd been shot on the TV news, 'Look North'. I don't watch ITV on account of the fact that I like the BBC and I thought, well, there goes my package holiday. I was going to Spain. I always go to Spain in November. It's not too hot then." Liz Humby was a large-boned woman, a little overweight, puffy about the face, with the sort of hair that a hairdresser would have difficulty doing something with. It was pale coloured, almost grey, and hung on her head like a mop. She sat in the chair in the front room of her small council house in Clemanthorpe with her arms hanging limply by her side. She spoke a flat monotone and seemed uninterested in the half-dozen flies buzzing about the shade the room provided from the heat and the light of the June day outside. The curtains, being half shut, exacerbated the gloom. Hennessey rapidly formed the opinion that the woman was living a small life and was shutting herself away even from that. He put her age as being about forty, about the same age as her husband, the slippery Major Hargrave, presently a member of the Yorkshire squirearchy and living a very well set existence.

"How long has it been going on?"

"About three years. I like Spain. I like Benidorm. I go a lot."

"So I see." Hennessey cast his eye about the room; drab, spartan, unclean, untidy, but "lifted" here and there by a coaster or a framed photograph or an ornamental dagger, all of which had "Benidorm" printed on them.

"How did it start?"

"Ossler, he came knocking on my door so he did, right out of the blue. First time I'd met him and he didn't beat about the bush, he didn't beat about the bush at all didn't Ossler, no . . . anyway, tells me my husband was alive."

"You believed your husband to be deceased?"

"Dead, you mean? Well he disappeared didn't he? Walked out one day and didn't come back. There was no row nor nothing, he just went, didn't he? Left everything, birth certificate, passport, driving licence . . . police thought I'd done him in . . . searched the house and had dogs sniffing about the garden. I mean, the neighbours . . ."

"That's just routine," Hennessey said, reassuringly as he saw Mrs Humby as being a little personality inside a very large body and as a woman he too would find some difficulty in living with, not doubting that eventually he too would probably have walked out of her life.

"I just thought he was dead . . . after a while he didn't come back, I thought he was dead, murdered even. I mean there was no arguing . . . I always did what he wanted, my mother said that. She said marriage is like riding a horse, one has to sit in front holding the reins and the other's got to ride behind holding on as best she can. So I always sat behind and let him do the steering and that was what my mother said to do, so there's no reason for him to leave me. So I thought he'd been murdered or had an accident and his body lying somewhere, even after all these years, oh yes."

"And that does happen as well," Hennessey said and paused as an ice-cream van drove down the street, its bells loudly chiming 'Greensleeves' and making all conversation impossible.

"Twice a day he comes," Liz Humby said, speaking as if hypnotised, staring straight ahead. "Once in the morning and once in the afternoon. This is the morning one."

"Yes," said Hennessey but managed to refrain from saying anything more caustic. Apart from his own self-respect which he wished to retain, he did after all want this dull woman's interesting information.

"But he wasn't dead, no he wasn't. I never knew what happened to him but Ossler, he came to my door and tells me I'm not a widow woman after all. Yes he did. Didn't like him much."

"Ossler?"

"My husband. Wasn't sorry he'd gone. Mind, now you mention it, I didn't like Ossler much either. Sort of creepy, slimy, slippery . . . no, didn't like him either. But Ossler tells me my husband isn't dead, tells me he's married, married a wealthy widow woman and lives in a grand house. Oh yes, a grand house. Showed me a photo."

"Of your husband?"

"No. I got plenty of them. No, of the house. Grand house. Ossler said my husband had done some work for him, putting up a fence or some such, he was a jobbing odd job man was my husband. That was when my husband was here, before he'd disappeared. That's how Ossler knew this address. Anyway, after my husband had been gone a year or two Ossler came to my door. My husband's alive, he said, and married to a wealthy woman called Hargraves . . . I think that's what he said. That meant he was a bigamist, that meant, oh yes. Me, I was all for going to the police but Ossler said 'no'. Ossler said we should blackmail him."

"Mrs Humby, I have to advise you that you may be about to incriminate yourself."

"I could get into trouble, I know that." Liz Humby continued to sit still, hands lightly by her side, eyes fixed on a point about three feet from her face. "But it doesn't matter. Ossler said he can't go to the police. Ossler said that the police can only act on a complaint. Ossler said that even if the police knew we was blackmailing him, they couldn't do anything unless he made a complaint, Ossler said."

"You're still admitting it . . ."

"Ossler said you have to find folk who can't go to the police, then the pennies just start to drop out of the sky." She continued to speak as though Hennessey's words hadn't reached her. "Except it was more than pennies."

"It was pounds?"

"Oh yes. Benidorm every year. In the autumn, cooler then. See, my husband had got involved with the cadet force as well as married to a wealthy woman. He'd lose everything."

122

"The army is important to your husband I take it?"

"Best years of his life, but he wasn't a regular soldier, he was in the Territorials. Put in a lot of time, more than just the weekends and one night a week. It was all he had. Then he left, resigned over a dispute, regretted it but they wouldn't let him back in. If he tells you he was in the regular army and resigned because he didn't make staff college, he's telling the lie he tells anyone who'll listen. He lived with me in this house, he earned money by jobbing but each weekend and one evening a week and whenever else he could, he was a major in the British Army. Never took me to any of the parties they had in the officers' mess though. He never did that. Never could understand that because I always rode behind like my mother said I had to do. Anyway, I left it all to Ossler and each month I'd get a brown envelope in the post, just money, nothing else. I live on benefit and that doubled my income. It meant . . ."

"You could go to Benidorm, I know. But it was immoral money. You may still yet be prosecuted."

Then Liz Humby showed a sign of a spark. She looked directly at Hennessey and said "Look at me. *Look* at me. What have I got to fear from prosecution? I'd be better off in gaol, company, free food, no bills . . . if they fine me I'll not pay it, to make them send me to gaol." Then she seemed to "click" back into her hypnotic trance and stare at a fixed point about three feet in front of her eyes. "That's my little honey pot all dried up. You know that's the high point of my life. Double money for about eighteen months."

"Does, or did, your husband own a gun?"

"He didn't need to. He was a soldier, well . . ."

"But he'd know how to use a gun?"

"I should think so. Do you think he shot Ossler?"

123

"We're open-minded about it. Do you think he's capable of that sort of action?"

"Well, he's capable of walking out on me . . . that takes something. Oh yes."

Hennessey thought that there was a look of resignation about the man. Yellich thought the man had a look about him as though he had woken up to find that he wasn't dreaming, which he further thought was probably not too far from the truth. The fourth man in the room was a well-built, pot-bellied, bearded man whose appearance both Hennessey and Yellich thought most un-lawyer like, but who had presented at the inquiry desk and introduced himself to the constable as "Crowther, duty solicitor". The red recording light glowed warmly and the twin cassettes rotated silently.

"Nothing to say," said Hargrave. "Except . . . except the one thing you want me to do, which is to confess."

"Confess?" Hennessey raised his eyebrows. He didn't expect it to be as easy as this. "You shot Ossler?"

"No." Hargrave smiled and shook his head. "No . . . I didn't do that . . . the thought did cross my mind, that happened . . . but I didn't do that. I can well imagine that you wished you had a tenner for every felon who said that to you, but in this case, it's true. I didn't do it. Glad somebody did though. Ossler got what was coming to him. Blew my cover, though. I was well dug in and then Ossler came, held on to an impossible position, someone 'offed' him and there I was on dead ground. What else can I do but confess I'm a bigamist?"

"So, Ossler was blackmailing you?"

"Yes . . . The Vale is a small place really. If you belong

124

to the right set, there's only so many hunts or golf clubs you can belong to. I left the army . . ."

"The Territorials?"

Hargrave gave Hennessey a pained look. "Polished your kit, haven't you?"

"It's my job, uncovering the truth. Over the years I've gotten to be quite good at it."

"Well, I've nothing to lose anyway. No strategic retreat for me from here. Yes, I'd finished with the Territorials, resigned in a temper but they didn't want me so I couldn't go back. Only held a temporary commission. I wanted a Queen's Commission but I never got one. I've no skills, no bits of paper . . . survived by jobbing. Put up a fence for Ossler round his house Thundercliffe Grange, would you believe. It wasn't even a 'grange' it was a new build bungalow with a little bit of a garden."

"Quite a lot of garden, but hardly a grange, I'll grant you."

"At least he didn't call it the Taj Mahal, and that I can tell you would not have been beyond Ossler. He was a swine of a man. I saw the way he spoke to his wife and secretary . . . I tell you, the dogs had a better life than they did."

"Got to know the dogs, did you, Mr Hargrave?"

"Well enough . . . no . . . now wait a minute, if someone got past the dogs to reach Ossler and you think . . . oh . . . no . . . sorry, you're way, way off . . ."

"It would explain it, though, wouldn't it?" Hennessey spoke softly. "Because, you see, someone did get past the dogs, and being a dog owner myself, I know how difficult that can be, especially when these dogs are Alsatians. I wouldn't mess with one, let alone two."

Hargrave smiled. "Neither would I."

"You wouldn't have to. If they knew you."

"But I didn't."

"We'll come back to that."

"There's nothing to come back to."

"The blackmail. Tell me about that?"

"Well, I jobbed for Ossler, donkey work really, each night I went back to my little council flat and that brain-dead lump I'd married . . . me . . . I'd been a major in the British Army, the high point of my life . . . well, one day I just said 'I'm off'. I said that. I just walked out to start fresh somewhere else . . . but I wouldn't leave York. It's my home town. I wouldn't be happier anywhere else . . . I like the history of the place, things like that. It makes me feel good that tourists come to visit my town."

"Yes . . . yes."

"Well, I'd let my appearance go just before I walked out on 'the lump' and so I cleaned myself up and bought a sports jacket from the Oxfam shop just in case 'the lump' should see me in the city centre, but I needn't have bothered really, you know she'd trip over the Minster and she wouldn't notice it. I bet I could go up to her now and ask directions and she wouldn't recognise me. But I didn't go to my old haunts, I went where the money drinks. By then I'd wangled a position in the cadet force, not back in the Terriers but close enough, and I was calling myself 'Major' again. Met Mrs Hargraves. She was a widowed lady and there was a spark between us. I told her I was single . . . once I had told her that lie, there was no return and I wouldn't have been in this mess."

"So what happened?"

"We got married. Simple as that. There's no record linkage you see, all I had to do was sign a form declaring that I was free to marry and Bob's your uncle. I did that because I wanted her money, and she has money all right, pots of it. If only . . . I imagine you could do with a tenner for everyone who said that to you as well."

"I wouldn't go hungry, that's for sure."

"Anyway, we got married. Simple civil ceremony but we turned convention on its head and I took her name. It helped me separate from 'the lump' and she wanted it that way anyway. You see, there was some needle between her and her in-laws. I don't know the story but I think she wasn't as 'top drawer' as her in-laws would have wanted for their son but you wouldn't think that now. She's really let those shire county mannerisms rub off on her. Anyway, her father was a deckhand on the trawlers, her in-laws owned part of the trawler fleet as well as a lot of land round Scarborough. You get the idea?"

"Aye."

"Anyway, twenty years of marriage, no children and her better half falls off his horse when he's chasing a fox much to the mirth of the hunt saboteurs who witnessed the accident. But even they stopped laughing when it was discovered he'd broken his neck. So she was a widow, lotta money, lotta ownership of the Hargrave fortune . . . their only son had married an 'oik', no heirs, so said 'oik' was set to inherit the lot. It was really the end of the Hargraves. Anyway, when they heard she was getting married again they thought 'well at least our name's ours again even if she has got half the rest of it'. Everything that wasn't their son's they bequeathed to very distant relatives you see, but she had a surprise up her sleeve."

"She kept the name?"

"In one. So me, another 'oik' from the council estate,

who teaches children to drill on Saturdays, also became a Hargrave. Not just any Hargrave, but one of the Scarborough Hargraves whose lands had been held by the same family since the dissolution of the monasteries. Didn't put me on their Christmas card list though," he added with a smile.

Hennessey said nothing but retained eye contact.

"For a while living was good, big house, plenty of money, position in society, what more could a man want? It all began to fall apart when Ossler, with his pushy nature and new money, started banging on the door of the Vale's social life. Joined the golf club, recognised me in the bar, came over and said "Hello . . . what are *you* doing here . . . like I was the dirt, not him. Then a week later he phoned me at home, he didn't waste time . . . he told me to meet him."

"He told you?"

"He told me. Told me to come to his house so I borrowed my wife's second car and drove to his house. His wife and secretary were there so he took me into a little office next to the room where his secretary works and he sat down. I stood. He said, 'Right Hargrave, or do I call you Humby?' Then he went on about him being a professional blackmailer . . ."

"And he told you that he never put the squeeze on people who could go to the police and never asked for more than they could afford?"

Hargrave's jaw slackened. "Yes . . . why? Have you spoken to other victims of his?"

"Well, let's just say we've grasped the gist of his operation. But do go on."

"Well, then he dropped a photograph of me and 'the lump' on our wedding day . . . you know all that day . . . all that day of my wedding there was a little voice in my head saying 'don't do it . . . don't do it' . . . but I went ahead and did it. Then I'd said the words and signed the papers and the little voice said, 'Nice one, squirrel, that's you well and truly stuffed now isn't it, Sunshine? And you can't say you weren't warned.' Then I stuck it out until I couldn't take it any more, her . . . that voice . . . that nothing to come home to to . . . and so I walked out, saying I was going to the pub, but when I came to the pub I just kept on walking and that same little voice spoke to me again and this time it said, 'Nice one, son, nice one, now just keep walking.' And after a few weeks in dingy lodgings, I met and married and all was very well until I bumped into Ossler at the golf club. Then all was suddenly very not well. Very not well at all."

"Then what?"

"Wanted money, didn't he? Came straight to the point. Admitted it was a dangerous game. Told me he'd lost his first wife to an 'angry client', called his victims his 'clients', in a case of mistaken identity, something to do with a duffel coat. That was what the new house and the dogs and the fence were all about, apparently. She had stopped a bullet that was meant for him, so he said. Anyway, he said all he had to do was send copies of my first marriage certificate, conveniently supplied by our mutual friend 'the lump', no doubt, for some modest percentage or a one-off payment, to the Cadet Corps Commission and to my wife, Mrs Hargrave. Then that was me shot, no job, no pension, no marriage."

"Meaning no big house and use of the second car, rather than no marriage?"

"If you like."

"Well I'm London born, Mr Hargrave, but to take an expression that you have just used, the culture of this

129

county has rubbed off on me and I have learned to call a spade a spade."

"If not a bloody shovel, that's even more Yorkshire."

"If you like. But please . . ."

"Well, I told him I hadn't got a lot . . . my wife has it all. It was hers before our marriage and it was hers after our marriage. I'm really there to fill up the vacant chair next to her in the golf club cocktail bar . . . we . . . well, we have separate bedrooms you see."

"I see."

"Oh, it's better. Me and 'the lump' had to share a bed. Can you imagine what that was like?"

"Just carry on, please."

"Eventually he said that he'd take my salary. All of it. I'd do the job but survive by living off my wife. It was that . . ."

"Or the open ground?"

"As you say, and we all know what happens to a soldier who finds himself on open ground? So that's how it was for about . . . nearly two years. So it's over . . . 'thy sins will seek thee out'. I've finished now . . . nothing to live for . . . so what can I do?"

"You can confess to blowing his brains out . . . the worm turned, as they say. After two years of working for nothing, two years of wondering if he'd plant you on the open ground you fear so much, just out of spite . . . any man can take just so much . . . that constant fear of exposure. You knew his house . . . its weak points . . . the gravel drive was pretty well useless when there was a lawn to walk on, the dogs would welcome you with wagging tails . . . the cadet corp's armoury . . . and it would be a simple matter to make a couple of dumdum bullets which would disintegrate on impact, and which couldn't then be matched to a particular gun barrel, so you could bob the gun back into the armoury and no one would be any the wiser. And you don't have an alibi. All that motivation, that clear, obstacle-free road, and no alibi. You know non-alibis can be broken as well as alibis."

Hargrave's eyes narrowed. His complexion paled. Hennessey saw it and said, "If we can place you somewhere on the Sunday evening, with a car and in striking distance of Ossler's house, then you've got some explaining to do, having already told us that you were at home all Sunday evening."

"I didn't kill Ossler," said in a slow but very controlled voice

"Things are looking bad for you, Mr Hargrave. Very bad."

"You can believe what you want to believe, and you can float any theory under the sun." Hargrave spoke in the same controlled voice, but also revealed a hard, menacing edge to his personality. "But both you and I know that the Crown Prosecution Service will only run with what it thinks it can run with. And that means what it can prove. So, if you think I killed Ossler, fine . . . all you've got to do now is convince a jury and I'll collect a life sentence."

Hennessey paused. "You've danced this dance before haven't you, Mr Hargrave? Or perhaps I should call you Humby. Do you have any other aliases? I've notices aliases are like that, once a person gives himself one alias he or she tends to like the idea. It has been my experience that if a person has one alias, he's likely got five or six."

"Or she."

"Or she."

"Well, that's for me to know and for you to find out."

"Don't be too cocksure. I've known the CPS to run with less than that beginning to stick to you. Haven't you, Sergeant?"

"Oh, much less," nodded Yellich. "Much less."

"That's too near to intimidation for me to be comfortable with," Crowther said, speaking for the first time since the interview commenced, when he had spoken only to give his name as being present in the room – as dictated by the procedures of the Police and Criminal Evidence Act.

"Very well." Hennessey leaned forward. "Mr Hargrave, aka Humby, you can make it hard for yourself or you can make it easy for yourself. One or the other. Your choice."

"I didn't kill Ossler."

"Plead guilty. It'll be reflected in the length of your sentence."

"Coercion," Crowther said, flatly.

Silence.

"This is not going anywhere." Crowther spoke with quiet authority. "We have had no break for refreshment, though I concede none was requested, but now I have to request that you either charge Mr Hargrave aka Humby, or release him pending further inquiries."

"Do you have an address to be released to, Mr Hargrave?" Hennessey asked.

"I really don't know." Hennessey shook his head slowly. "I've got two wives, but I can't live with either. Not now. No friends. No relatives."

"So, you are of no fixed abode?"

"I suppose I am. About an hour ago my home was one of the most prestigious houses in the Vale."

"Very well. William Hargrave, or Humby, I arrest you

132

in connection with the murder of Nathan Ossler on Sunday last. You do not have to say anything but it may harm your defence if you do not mention when questioned something you later rely on in court. Anything you do say may be given in evidence."

In Hennessey's pigeon hole was a fax from the forensic science laboratory in Wetherby. The firearms section regretted it could be of little use in respect of the samples of bullet pieces sent for analysis, other than to confirm that it was of a .22 calibre and clearly fragmented on impact suggesting that it had been "doctored" into a "dumdum" bullet. It would not be possible to match it to the barrel from which it was fired.

Hennessey filed the report pondering the strangely unscientific use of the word "doctored", especially in an official communication. He thought that the weekend was probably arriving a little early for one stressed-out government scientist.

Hennessey and Yellich drove out to the Hargrave house at Bishop Wilton, pleasantly well set in the Yorkshire Wolds. Yellich drove. Hennessey in the front passenger seat, found time to reflect upon the beauty of the area he was privileged to work in, gentle, rolling countryside, wide, distant skyline, fields under crops or given to grazing, with the landscape broken up here and there with stands of woodland. The Hargrave house was on the edge of the village, a solid, four square building, probably, Hennessey thought, dating from the mid-eighteenth century. It was covered in Virginia creeper and stood in well-tended grounds. Although Hennessey would never leave his house in Easingwold

133

because that would involve leaving Jennifer, he did on occasion and only in his fantasy, find himself coveting other people's property and this was one such occasion. The Hargrave house, he decided, was a very serious pile of stone, very serious indeed.

Clarissa Hargrave "received" the police officers in her drawing-room. she lay in a silk and richly embroidered trouser suit on a *chaise-longue* and smoked cigarettes, held in a long cigarette holder. Hennessey saw then why she could find William Humby or Hargrave attractive. He was, after all, slim, muscular, and at least twenty years her junior.

"Police?" She spoke in a harsh voice which both officers assumed to have been created by years of cigarette smoking. The room, heavily decorated and furnished to the point of "clutter", yet expensively so, gold candlesticks on carved oak tables, smelled heavily of stale tobacco smoke. The ornate ceiling was stained yellow.

"Detective Chief Inspector Hennessey. Detective Sergeant Yellich. I'm Hennessey."

"Please," she waved an imperious arm in a wide silk sleeve, "do take a seat and tell me to what I owe the pleasure of your company."

She may, reflected Hennessey, have been a trawler deckhand's daughter, but she had clearly absorbed all the mannerisms of her in-laws. He and Yellich sat in deep armchairs which Hennessey thought dated from the inter-war period. He had seen the like in junk shops and had watched as they eventually became valuable antiques.

"Mrs Hargrave, we have this morning arrested your husband in connection with the murder of Nathan Ossler. There are some questions we have to put to you."

"Good for him." Clarissa Hargrave drew deeply on the cigarette in the holder.

"You don't seem surprised?"

"I am surprised in that I didn't think the little twerp had it in him. Just goes to show how you can be married to someone and not know him at all." Hennessey thought, "you don't know the half of it, madam, not the half of it", but kept the words in his head.

"Well, well, well. I read about Ossler, getting shot, of course. So my husband did it . . . he avenged me. Do you know what Ossler did to me in the bar of the golf club? Poured beer down my front, not over my dress, but inside my dress . . . the effrontery. I was the talk of the golf club . . . still am. So Little William has something about him after all, he's really worth more than just standing there looking neat giving off essence of man. Honour is satisfied."

"We have not yet the proof we really need."

"But you suspect him enough to arrest him? That's good enough for me . . . that invertebrate Ossler got what has been long coming to him. He was a pushy man, not at all universally popular. I told my husband that I wouldn't be happy until I saw him dead."

"You said that?"

"I said a lot of things that night, but the thrust of my emotions was that I wanted Ossler dead, I wanted his death to be both slow and immeasurably painful. So a bullet in the head was too quick, but you can't have it all." She drew on the cigarette, burning it to the butt. She unscrewed the filter out of the cigarette holder, tossed it into a huge cut glass ashtray which was half full of similar filters, took a cigarette from a gold-plated case, pushed it into the holder and lit it with a gold-plated lighter. "I dare say it's obvious what my

135

doctor has advised me to do, but it's my only pleasure and at my age . . . so—"

"Your husband had a motivation to shoot Ossler, you say?"

"Of course, to keep me . . . to keep this house . . . this standard of living . . . men do that for me, you know. My late husband fought a duel to satisfy my honour, do you know that? A real duel, not, fortunately to the death, but a duel none the less. A man dared to imply that I married my dear husband for his money, not for my deep abiding love for him, my origins being a little more humble than my husband's, you see."

"Ah . . ." Hennessey nodded. Yellich sat with his hands held together, looking a trifle uncomfortable, and responded to Mrs Hargrave's explanation with a brief smile.

"He wouldn't retract what he said and so a duel was fought in the form of a bare-knuckle boxing match in the grounds of this house at dawn, all proper, ten three-minutes rounds, with seconds . . . I sat on a chair and watched it as the sun rose. Two men bloodying themselves for the sake of my honour . . . the romance . . . my husband fighting to defend my honour . . . how many women can say that?"

"Not many."

"Not at the cusp of the millennium. The twenty-first century has dawned and here am I, probably the only woman in all England who can say that a duel was fought over the question of her honour. Of course my husband would kill for me, for the sake of my honour. I'll have to divorce him now that he's been stupid enough to be caught, he'll be in prison for a long time now, so he's no use to me."

"Mrs Hargraves, where were you on Sunday evening?"

"Why? Am I under suspicion? How exciting. Will I be

arrested and have my rights read to me or is it only the Americans who do that?"

"Just answer the question."

"Out."

"Out?"

"Yes, it means not in. Not at home. Not in residence. I was out. You see, it's the state of not being in. Like a man who plays cricket, he's in until he's out. And when all those who are in are out, then the side that's been out goes in."

"Yes, I've got a tea towel with that on as well, Mrs Hargraves," Hennessey said icily. "Where were you when you were out?"

"With my girlfriends. I have a very cast-iron alibi. We played bridge at Lucy Bingham's house. Tonya Villiers and Miranda Courtney-Smyth were there too. They'll vouch for me." She dictated Lucy Bingham's phone number and Yellich wrote it in his notepad.

"And your husband was at home when you were out?"

"He was at home when I left, and he was at home when I returned shortly after midnight, but he'd gone out and returned in the interim."

Silence. A clock ticked. Clarissa Hargraves pulled deeply on the cigarette holder and smiled as though she knew she had said something of significance and was enjoying the game.

"The flower was crushed, you see."

"The flower?"

"I permit my husband restricted use of my second car. He's allowed two hundred miles per month. My maid tells me when he has used up his allowance upon which he must surrender the keys to me. It is handed back to him on the first day of the next month. We are now near the beginning of June, he has a few miles to play with. I thought he might sneak out and so I did what I always do on such occasions, I plucked a flower from the garden and placed it under the rear wheel of the car. When I returned the car was in the same place, almost, but the flower had been crushed. So he'd gone for a little drive, not far, but the bonnet of the car was still warm. He would have left shortly after I left and returned . . . well how long does it take for a car's bonnet to cool down completely, an hour, half an hour? No rain or cold weather to cool it down . . . a warm June night. I returned at half past midnight . . . there was still a slight trace of heat in the bonnet, very slight."

"It's a small car?"

"A Ford Fiesta."

"A small engine, it wouldn't generate a lot of heat."

"No . . . the Bentley, the bonnet of the Bentley remains warm for an hour after the car has remained parked, longer sometimes, depending on the weather."

"The bonnet of a Ford Fiesta would cool within fifteen minutes," Yellich offered.

"So he could have returned as late as quarter past midnight." Hennessey turned to Yellich.

"It would give him the time, boss."

"Oh good." Clarissa Hargrave grinned. "Do I sense the net closing on my husband?"

"No comment. But he told us he was in the house all Sunday evening."

"Well the little toad's lying to you. The second car moved and only he was in a position to drive it. He has a capacity to lie, it's part of his nature. He told me he'd been in all evening as well, I didn't tell him about the flower under the wheel of the car."

"You didn't challenge him?"

"No . . . but I did add it to a certain little list I am keeping, the sum of which is already greater than the constituent parts and one day I shall drop it in front of his little self when I want something special. Generally he does my least bidding, but occasionally I need a little something to hold over him . . . he's scared of losing me you see, men are, and I like things on my terms at all times. We married on my terms, we live on my terms, and that's how I like it. I learned the art of that from my first husband, he tended to do things on his terms."

"What time did you leave home on Sunday evening?" Hennessey asked, bringing the interview back on track.

"About eight p.m. I returned after midnight and William was waiting up for me like the dutiful Labrador he is and he told me he'd been in all evening watching television. He told me what he'd watched but he could have got that information from the TV guide."

"Easily."

"But I'd already checked the flower so I went up the stairs, had a shower and went to bed feeling very smug. I do like having things to hold over my husband, my mother told me that. Mr father was a burly deckhand and my mother was a small fisherwoman but she had him jumping through hoops. It's all about knowledge you know, it's all about knowing things that he doesn't know you know. Knowledge is power."

"But your information is interesting." Hennessey leaned forwards. "Apart from anything else, it means we were right to detain him."

"What other reason could you have to detain him?"

"Well . . ." Hennessey said quietly, as beside him he

felt Yellich stiffen. "You see we have found out that your husband may have had another motive for murdering Ossler other than to avenge your indignity . . . we know that Ossler was blackmailing your husband."

Clarissa Hargrave's jaw sagged. "Why?"

Her eventual scream, high pitched and piercing, brought the maid running to the room, by which time Clarissa Hargrave was standing up, fists clenched by her side, screaming at the ornate ceiling. After explaining to the maid that her employer had had a little bad news, Hennessey and Yellich let themselves out of the huge house. As they walked from the front door towards their car, Clarissa Hargrave's scream was clearly audible and showed no sign of abating, penetrating the interior of the officers' car and following them as they drove towards the gate and the road back to York.

"So, where were you?" Hennessey asked William Hargrave. Yellich and another duty solicitor were present on this occasion, a slightly built but very serious minded woman called "Miss Smith". Hennessey at least found her serious minded and utterly humourless, having met her on previous occasions. The red recording light glowed, twin cassettes spun silently, slowly. "You're getting yourself in deeper and deeper . . . all you can do now is to come clean."

"Did you tell her why Ossler was blackmailing me?"

"Yes. We had to. We couldn't keep that sort of information from her."

"How did she take it?"

"As you'd expect."

Hargrave's jaw set firm. "She can cheat but she can't be cheated . . . she has to be in control but she wasn't in control at all. No more easy life for me, but at least I was there on my terms all the time . . . no, I can imagine she had known happier moments in her life."

"So, where were you?"

"I wonder what's going to happen to me now?"

"Sunday night!" Hennessey slapped his palm on the desk top. "That's all we are interested in. Sunday night. You drove from your home to Ossler's house and you shot him. Yes?"

"No."

"Look, you've got no alibi, you've got a strong motive and you've got the means. Even with your alibi the CPS would have run with it, now your alibi's shot, you have no defence. Best you come clean."

"Well that's where you're wrong. My alibi's not shot, my alibi's as strong as strong can be. I was with my girlfriend."

Hennessey groaned. "You'll excuse my cynicism, Mr Hargrave or Humby . . ."

"I was with my girlfriend." Hargrave spoke calmly. "I was with my girlfriend. But I can't tell you her name."

"That's the sort of alibi we get from delinquent youths."

"I can't tell you her name."

"Because she doesn't exist."

"Oh, she exists all right . . . we met through a dating agency . . . you might have seen it advertised . . . Dangerous Liaisons . . . it puts people in touch with each other who are in a bad marriage but are holding on for one reason or another, children usually . . . but in my case, it's good living, and who want a secret lover to help them, help us, get through, one day at a time until we have a rendezvous."

"So tell us her name. It's in your interest. If she exists."

Hennessey pressed. "If not, you're in deeper. We'll have to keep you here."

"Keep me here. It's safer. Nowhere to go anyway. So it's cheaper as well."

"This interview," Hennessey said coldly, "is terminated at sixteen forty hours."

Hennessey sat at his desk writing up the content of the interview with Hargrave, adding that he was not losing sight of the possibility of Nigel West as a suspect. Presently he became aware of someone standing to his left. He looked up. Commander Sharkey stood in the door frame. Hennessey thought he looked worried. He'd seen Sharkey look like this before and he knew what was pressing on Sharkey's mind.

"There's nothing to worry about is there, George?"

"Nothing at all, sir."

"Had all I want of that in Hong Kong you know. The entire force was run on it. Just don't want it here. Nothing like that with us, not here in York."

"Don't worry, sir," Hennessey smiled. "None of us want it either. Any indication of that and we'll all squeal like stuck pigs. Thanks again for the book."

"My pleasure. No hurry to return it."

Yellich didn't want to do it, but his wife had prevailed upon him. Being the secretary, he thought, was sufficient, but Sara had pressed and prodded and eventually he had conceded and they hosted the York District Special Needs (Parents') Support Group in their home on a bi-monthly basis. Soon Yellich was able to admit that he enjoyed the evening. The other parents of children similar to Sam had, over the years, become their friends, and the children had become friends with each other. Usually it was "business", negotiating the Health Service maze and/or the Social Security maze, advice about parenting issues, but occasionally a day trip to the coast had been organised.

On this occasion, a psychologist had agreed to talk to the group for no fee about an issue which was pressing on two other sets of parents in the group whose children were older than Sam, but which issue Yellich and his wife knew was ahead of them: sexuality and learning difficulties. It was the worrying minefield of issues when juvenile mentality is mixed with developing adult urges and attraction. Not easy. That meeting was well attended and at the end, over tea and biscuits, the parents each agreed that the meeting had succeeded in allaying fears and immense was the gratitude shown to the young female psychologist who seemed to Yellich to be mollified by it all.

Hennessey sat with the woman at the long table in her dining kitchen. Upstairs the children ran to and fro and squabbled about the use of "their" bathroom. They didn't speak, but held hands and gazing into each other's eyes, and he saw again how warm those eyes were, as warm as he remembered Jennifer's eyes being. He had returned home to Easingwold, eaten, exercised Oscar, phoned his son – just to retain contact, as had developed their relationship, their father and son friendship. He had then made another brief phone call, packed an overnight bag and driven to Skelton, to a half-timbered house in the village, a gravel drive, a double garage which he knew housed, if not "homed" a 1947 Riley, the beloved possession of the owner of the property, the red

143

and white car in pristine, as new condition, being the only car ever owned by her beloved father.

"It's gone quiet," the woman said softly. "Peace in our time."

"They've settled quickly tonight," Hennessey replied.

"Diane and Fiona are tired, they've been at the stables all evening getting Samson ready for the show at the weekend. Dan's just tired."

"Ah . . . my great rival in love." Hennessey squeezed her hand. "I worked out that I'm eighth in your life in terms of importance. I humbly take my place behind three children, a career, a horse and two rabbits, lop-eared at that. But I'm pleased to be here. So, so pleased. It's been a long time . . ."

"For both of us." Louise D'Acre returned the squeeze. "Shall we go up?"

Six

In which Hennessey meets a timid woman in a large house and a second suspect moves into the frame for the murder of Nathan Ossler.

"H e went to the gun club. He's gone to the gun club." Hennessey's heart missed a beat. "Excuse me?"

"The gun club," the timid woman repeated. "He's gone there." She sat stiffly in the chair, occasionally glancing out of the twelve foot high window pane at the children playing in the garden. "They're convalescing," she said by means of explanation. "Summer cold. But they're better now . . . back to school tomorrow for the last few days of term. A little bit of peace before the summer mayhem, but I dare say I'll miss them when they're gone. What's that condition . . . empty nest syndrome? But summer in France and then ten blessed peaceful weeks of the Christmas term."

"The gun club?" Hennessey repeated. "I didn't know he had an interest in guns?"

"Oh he has. He was there on Sunday evening. Stayed late. Got back after midnight."

"Really? Confess I was surprised when he wasn't at his school. I would have thought that like all teachers, he was committed from nine to four p.m. . . . but I was told he'd gone out for the morning."

"Well, headmasters are more akin to managers than teachers, he can leave the hour-to-hour running of the school to the deputy head, or to the heads of departments if he needs to attend meetings with the senior people in the Education Department for example."

"That I can understand, but to leave school to go to the gun club . . . it's not a very professional attitude."

The woman shrugged. "You'll have to ask my husband that . . . but the end of term, a few days of soft pedalling before the summer break . . . he probably thought he could afford to take an hour off."

"And the gun club is open at this hour of the day?"

"It's like a golf club. The premises are always open, there's often another few members in the bar or coffee shop. The range is accessible to fire off a few rounds. It's a recent interest of his . . ."

"Recent?"

"A few years, as opposed to a lifelong interest."

"I see, but interesting, nonetheless."

"They can't have handguns any more . . . but the passion for handguns hasn't gone away and I have to suspect quite a few handguns haven't been surrendered."

"I confess you and I are of like mind on that point, Mrs West," Hennessey smiled. "You wouldn't be suspecting that your husband is in possession of one such weapon?"

She shook her head. "I have no reason to suspect it."

"But he could have one?"

"Oh yes . . . he could . . . as I told you." She shuffled nervously.

"Point taken." Hennessey relaxed in the chair. Nigel

146

West was not at home and Hennessey's initial annoy-
ance at West's absence had evaporated once he sensed
the opportunity to gather a little background information
on him; the headmaster with a photograph of part of the
University of Cambridge on his study wall, when by all
accounts he should be a gym teacher with a certificate from
Derwent Teacher Training College. He asked. "How long
have you been married?"

"Eleven years."

"So you didn't meet at university?"

"Do I look that old?" She smiled nervously. "My husband
is quite a lot older than me. I'm in my early thirties, Mr West
is forty-eight."

"Nearly twenty years."

"Yes, nearly." Another timid, apologetic smile. "We met
at school . . . Mr West's school, I was a probationer, he
was then the Head of English. We took up with each other
when I finished my probationary year. Mr West decided
that I should move to another school so that we could carry
on our relationship a little more discreetly." She seemed to
Hennessey to be very admiring of her husband, though he
was already finding the sycophantic reference to her husband
as "Mr West" tiring, in the extreme. "He went to university."
She added, "Cambridge. He took an upper second."

"Yes, I know. I've met your husband."

"Oh . . . I only went to college, teacher training college.
I'm what is called 'timetable fodder' in the profession.
We get the bad timetable, least motivated, most disruptive
classes . . . I'm glad I got out. I married out." She gave
another long glance at the children. "A wife and mother
with a home to manage, that's all I ever wanted really, right
from when I was little with a doll's house." She returned

147

her attention to Hennessey. "And that's what I've got. I'm a lucky woman. A lovely house too."

Hennessey glanced round the large room. "It's a lovely house."

"It used to be the parsonage. It's difficult to heat in winter."

"I can imagine."

"In winter we hibernate in the kitchen. But in the summer, as you see . . . it's a lovely house."

"Your husband is not a Yorkshire man?"

"No. His family roots are in Bedfordshire."

"He attended local schools?"

"Good heavens no . . . I'm the council brat in this marriage. Mr West went to Taunton."

"Taunton?"

"A public school. Not quite up there with Eton and Harrow and places like that . . . what are they, the nine great public schools in England . . . but quite pukka just the same."

"Oh, I'm sure. I went to a council school in Greenwich. It got pulled down to make way for a block of flats. I'm a bit sorry about that I confess, I envy people who can revisit their school, especially when they're in the decline of life. I wasn't particularly happy at school, but when it was demolished I felt as though I'd been cast adrift."

"I can understand that," she nodded sympathetically. "But, well what do you want to see Mr West for?"

"Nothing to worry about. Just routine questions. He might be able to assist with inquiries. You only have the two children?"

"Yes. They're enough really. I wanted more but Mr West said that that would be bad for his prospects . . . he said a nuclear family looked better . . . a large family invites prejudice, so we stopped at two. I had an operation . . . Mr West insisted."

"You . . . *he* insisted?"

"Oh yes. Mr West is in charge."

Hennessey said nothing but he was getting a strong feel of the West household. All done on Mr West's terms, all on his say so. A man like that would need a timid creature like this for a partner, so Hennessey pondered, and again, knew why he had enjoyed his career in the police: "it pays nothing, but you see life and it's better than working", as is often heard said in the police club. "But your husband . . . we need to see him. Where is the gun club?"

"We?"

"I have two officers outside."

"You're going to arrest him!"

"Oh, I hope not," Hennessey smiled. "But sometimes people are not as co-operative as we'd like . . ."

"He won't like you going to the gun club looking for him . . . he's very particular about appearances."

"We can be diplomatic."

"I'm sure he'd rendezvous with you."

"That would be acceptable. If he's prepared to come to the police station directly . . . and I mean directly, tear himself away from his conversation or the firing range."

"I'll phone him." She stood up.

"I'll phone him." Hennessey also stood. "That's if I may use your phone?"

"It's in the hall." She sat down again, looking pale and frightened. "The number's in the book under 'G'," she added helpfully. "For gun, you see."

*   *   *

149

"Do you have an alibi for Sunday evening last?"

West didn't reply. He was smartly dressed and reeked of aftershave.

"Just say 'yes' or 'no' for the benefit of the machine."

West nodded his head. His eyes were steely cold.

"For the purposes of recording," Hennessey said, "Mr West nodded his head indicating an answer in the affirmative." He paused. "What is your alibi?"

"I was at the gun club."

"All evening?"

"No . . . I left early."

"How early?"

"I slipped away about nine p.m."

"Where were you around midnight?"

"I'd rather not say."

"Why? Because you were blowing Nathan Ossler's brains out at that moment?"

"No. I was with someone."

"Oh . . ." Hennessey groaned. "Not you as well."

The duty solicitor shot a disapproving glance at Hennessey.

"Sorry." Hennessey sighed. "Sorry, I shouldn't have said that . . . but you're not going to tell me that you've joined an organisation called 'Dangerous Liaisons'?"

"No," West smiled. "And I accept your apology. I've seen their adverts . . . I've even sent for information about their service. They're very discreet . . . introductions for attached people . . . they can't advertise widely. Some newspapers won't carry their ads."

"I can understand why."

"But what's wrong with it? If things are bad at home . . . why not . . . we only come this way once . . . why throw our life passage away on the wrong person?"

"Why indeed? But it's the underhand nature of the organisation that I find offensive . . . it would be more honest to leave home and petition for divorce, don't you think?"

"Perhaps, but there's a distinct advantage to hedging your bets. You run the risk of your affair being rumbled but it turns out you still have the little woman at home to return to. I also have children who'd suffer badly in a divorce. So, it's a risk worth taking, and there's the added thrill of the gamble . . . but mentioning Dangerous Liaisons . . . yes, you're on the right track."

"So who were you with?"

"A lady called Imogen Salt. You'll have to be discreet."

"Oh, we will."

"So you were with her at midnight on Sunday?"

"Well . . . no. We had a drink in a pub."

Hennessey paused. Beside him, Yellich shifted in his chair.

"The pubs shut at ten thirty on Sunday evenings."

"Yes," said West. "They do."

"Did you go somewhere else with Mrs Salt or did you part for the night?"

"We parted for the night."

"And the pub was in . . ."

"York. We were in the Golden Ball on Priory Street. A lovely pub . . . tucked away just right for a rendezvous."

"Yes . . . yes . . . so what time did you return home?"

"About midnight."

"After midnight, according to your wife."

West shot a glance, a glare, at Hennessey. "You've been to my house?"

"Yes. Twice in fact." Hennessey enjoyed the glare he'd

received from West. It gave a vivid insight into the man's personality.

"But today? You went to my home today?"

"Yes. We were looking for you. That's where I phoned you from. With your wife's permission, of course. So you parted from Mrs Salt at ten thirty in the evening in central York and arrived home at . . . after midnight. Do you know the location of the village of Strensall, Mr West?"

"Yes."

"It's about twenty minutes' drive from your house, would you say?"

"About. Yes."

"So you could be in Strensall at midnight and be at your home within twenty minutes?"

"Yes. I could have been. But I wasn't."

"So what did you do in the two hours between parting from Mrs Salt and arriving home?"

"I walked about. It was a lovely evening. I didn't want to go home to my wife, not so soon after parting from Mrs Salt." He eyed Hennessey coldly and held the edge of the table so tightly, so tightly that his knuckles whitened. "We are made for each other, Imogen and I . . . I needed time to think before I went back to my little wife whom I should never have married. I mean, wouldn't you?"

"This isn't about me, Mr West. When I called on the school the day before yesterday, we had a brief chat. You told me that you knew Ossler."

"Yes. Social climber that he is . . . or was. If you have a touch of class people like that clutch at your shirt tails. You learn to live with it."

"It was a little more complicated than that, wasn't it?"

"Was it?"

Hennessey cleared his throat. He saw the duty solicitor, Mr Crowther once again, glance curiously at Nigel West and he reflected on the curious fly-on-the-wall position of the duty solicitor during P.A.C.E. interviews. "Yes," he said, "it was significantly more than that. Can you tell me if Nathan Ossler perhaps ever described himself to you as a 'professional blackmailer'?"

West leaned back in his chair and bowed his head. His hands went up to his forehead, first one then the other. All he said was ". . . Oh."

"Couldn't go to the police, could you, Mr West?"

West remained silent, staring at the brown floor of the interview room.

"You couldn't because every salary cheque you've drawn for the last few years, ever since you invented a degree from Cambridge University has been an act of obtaining money by deception. You know it doesn't really matter if you went to a council school in Bedford and not to a prestigious public school, so long as you don't mislead or profit by that deception. But it does matter, it matters hugely, if you went to Derwent Teacher Training College; where you obtained the minimum qualifications necessary to teach secondary school level as a gym teacher, but invented university degrees sufficient to enable you to take a headship, and then accepted said headship. That's fraud, deception, a criminal matter. You even succeeded in withholding that from your wife."

West raised his head, but not to look at Hennessey, or Yellich, or to Mr Crowther, but beyond eye level, to the ceiling, as if wanting to be anywhere, anywhere in the world except interview room three in Micklegate Bar Police Station in the City of York. Eventually he lowered his head and looked at Hennessey and said, "I'd like a coffee. Something hot to sip."

Hennessey leaned to his right and held the on/off switch of the tape recorder and said. "This interview is halted at eleven fifteen a.m. to allow refreshments to be taken." He switched the machine off and the red "recording" light faded.

Coffee was produced in brown plastic cups from the vending machine. West and Mr Crowther remained in the interview room speaking in hushed tones, while Hennessey and Yellich stood in the corridor.

"Thoughts?" Hennessey asked.

"He can kill, boss." Yellich sipped his coffee. "He's got that killer instinct. He's solemn, very, very solemn. He can pull a trigger even if his life or the life of a loved one is not in danger. He'd walk quite calmly up to Ossler's house, get past the dogs with a tribute like a portion of fish and chips or a liquorice stick each, ice Ossler and walk away again. He's solemn enough. He has motive and no alibi . . . walking around York because it was a nice evening." Yellich smiled. "I mean, he could try the other one, that's the one with bells on."

Hennessey grinned, he hadn't heard that expression for a few years. "I confess, I'm leaning to that persuasion too, in fact for my money, he's more firmly in the frame than Mr Do-As-He's-Told Hargrave, despite Hargrave's access to firearms. I mean, Hargrave is more frightened of his old lady than he is a prison cell, in fact he's so frightened of the big, bad world, he forces us to lock him up."

"See, that's what I mean, boss." Yellich drained his plastic mug of the brown, tasteless liquid. "That's not a killer. This guy is. And he's in a gun club . . . we think that for every handgun that was handed in during the last amnesty, two were not. He'll have access to a gun as well, one of his own that no one else knows about."

"Well." Hennessey likewise drained his cup and tossed it into the wastepaper bin which sat on the corridor floor by the vending machine. "Let's let P.A.C.E. dictate the pace, see how far we get . . . softly, softly catchee monkey, as the felons would say."

Hennessey and Yellich re-entered the interview room, closing the door behind them, and sat down. Hennessey switched on the tape recorder, the red recording light glowed and the twin cassettes began to spin slowly. "The interview resumes after refreshments at eleven twenty-five a.m. I am Detective Chief Inspector George Hennessey, I am now going to ask the other persons present to identify themselves."

"Detective Sergeant Yellich."

"Crowther, duty solicitor of Crowther, Walsh, Smith & Chapple of Davygate, York."

"Nigel West of nowhere in particular. Not any more."

"Do I take that as a confession, Mr West?"

"Yes."

A silence, a tension seemed to be released from the room.

"How did you do it?"

"It?"

"Falsify your qualifications for one. How is it possible? Aren't they checked?"

"Yes, they're checked, but only once. Human frailties, an absence of built-in safeguards and random checks. It's a system that's open to abuse."

"As you have demonstrated."

"And I've been found out. I actually came to believe it after a while." He smiled. "I got to become convinced of

155

my own deception. I went away for weekends to Cambridge, stayed in bed and breakfast hotels and walked about the place until I knew the street layout and each individual college, each quad in each college. Once I had committed myself to the lie, I couldn't unlie, apart from leaving myself open to blackmail, which I never thought would happen, it meant I couldn't move to another local authority. You see, on joining a local authority, you have to show your qualifications, and prove your identity, often by showing your passport, but once in the authority, your identity and qualifications are assumed to have been checked."

"I see."

"I started work at a different school as the gym teacher and met the elitism and bullying that goes on in a school staff room. The teacher training college 'oiks' had to sit in the least comfortable chairs near the door, so it was up to us to answer the door each time someone knocked on it, while the graduates who would only talk to each other, walked past us and sat in the comfortable armchairs near the fire at the far end of the room."

"Got under your skin, I suppose?"

"Did rather, as did the jokes . . . in a culture that's orientated to academic success, being the gym teacher is to be the butt of everyone's humour . . . 'gym teachers are useful – they can lift things', 'if you can't teach, you can always teach gym', 'gym teachers always stand up because if they sit down it makes their brains sore.'"

"I begin to see your difficulty."

"I'm glad you understand, Chief Inspector. I'm glad you understand."

Hennessey remained silent. He did not, in fact, understand the problem as West had seen it. Other people make rewarding careers out of teaching gym, knowing that some children can only find self-expression through sport, others find achievement, others develop the sense of "team playing", so important in a competitive adult world. What Hennessey saw, rather, was the problem of a natural "control freak," so called. He saw the problem that a man who values status and appearance would have in being bottom of a pecking order. That was a problem he could understand.

"But occasionally," West began to speak more freely, thinking that in George Hennessey he had found a sympathetic ear, "occasionally, one of the graduates would deign to speak to me and I found out that I could hold my own, intellectually speaking – even win arguments. It was then that a notion began to take root."

"But you still couldn't change your qualifications?"

"There was a school, inner-city York, going through bad times, children running riot, staff leaving in droves, other teachers were asked to volunteer for posts, I saw my opportunity. Every gym teacher has a subsidiary academic subject which they teach in the last years of their career when they become too old to supervise soccer games in driving rain, which is earlier than you might think – rheumatism and arthritis arrive early in the life of sporty types, all that pounding that their bodies have to take."

"Or they voluntarily subject their bodies to."

"If you like. But anyway, I saw my chance. They were so desperate for staff I didn't think they'd cross-refer my internal application with my initial external application and so my teaching certificate from Derwent Teacher Training College became an upper second class honours degree in English Literature from the University of Cambridge. In

157

the very short interview I made all the right noises about 'wanting a challenge' and I got the job, largely because no one else wanted it. I knew that, but upon accepting the job I became a graduate teacher."

"And of Cambridge University no less."

"No less. But I was good at it. I lived up to the qualification and I was part of the staff group that turned that school around." West smiled. "You know the irony is that while I may have been obtaining money by deception, I actually earned it nonetheless. The Head of English at my present school became vacant, I applied for it. By then I'd been in the department about fifteen years. I was known, I was well known to be a Cambridge man, my original application as a probationer was well lost . . . I got the job. A few years after that the headship itself became vacant . . . another internal application, another interview, a little stiffer this time, but I was offered the post. A permanent post, mine until retirement. All I had to do was to hope that a random or even accidental reading of my file wouldn't expose my true qualifications or that another graduate of Derwent of my year group wouldn't walk into my school. I never thought that a school friend from my own school days would walk into my study and blackmail me."

"Is that what happened?"

"Yes." West paused. "Yes, I got a call, a phone call, my secretary put it through because the caller would only describe himself as a 'concerned parent' and would only speak to me. So I took the call and the man said that he was concerned about a matter of grave indiscretion that was being perpetrated by a member of staff at the school. Cunning that. He didn't say 'a member of your staff', but 'a member of staff'. That should have put me on my guard but sometimes things are only clear in hindsight."

"You couldn't have done anything anyway. He had you cold by then."

"He did, didn't he? Anyway, we made an appointment and he kept it, breezed in, cheerful, handshakes . . . sat down and said, 'Well, you've done all right for yourself'. I didn't recognise him. Then he said 'You don't recognise me, do you Compass?', that was my nickname at school, 'Compass West, is best'."

"Going from true north to magnetic north."

Hennessey nodded. "I was in the navy once."

"Well that's the origin. I was 'Compass' or 'Compy' all through school. Then he said 'It's me, Ossie, you remember. We bunked off together one afternoon and had to bend over for Tiffy the next day – three stripes each'. It was then I knew the game was up for me. I was never a close pal of Ossler's but I remember him as being a schemer, always into moneymaking schemes, always avoiding fights as well, slithery, slippery sort of boy, that was Nathan Ossler." West paused. "I mean the coincidence, he'd settled in the Vale. I thought I'd left him behind in Bedford with all the others."

"But there he was, in your study."

"There he was in my study, large as life with two press cuttings, one recent which showed a photograph of me when the local paper interviewed me about recent good results we'd had and gave my qualification as BA (Hons.) Cantab., and the other from a previous era when I'd helped pull a fellow student out of Lake Windermere after she got into difficulties and which clearly placed me at Derwent Teacher Training College. They were photocopies of course. I was there before him and said, 'How much do you want?'"

"And?"

"A lump sum twice my gross annual salary."

"Possible to meet?"

"Just, by means of a loan company, my house, the equity therein, my secure and well-paid position. Ossler . . . I can't tell you what that name does to me."

"When did he call on you?"

"About . . . about . . . six months ago . . . yes . . . at the beginning of the Easter term . . . snow on the ground, as I recall. I just sat there feeling the bottom fall out of my world and he also sat there, smiling, crowing about his success. Do you know how he got started? Ossler. Do you know how it all started for him?"

"Tell me."

"A bag snatch. Theft . . . he snatched a bag. It was on one of the London stations. Waterloo, I think. A woman had sold her house and had collected the proceeds in cash from her solicitor and was hoarding the money. That's big money."

"I'll say."

"Ossler was a petty thief hoping for a few knick-knacks he could sell to buy an evening in a pub. Makes it at the station, gets back to Bedford, he was still living at home then, forces it open in his dad's tool shed and . . . oh my . . . enough hard cash to buy a house in a London suburb and he was still only twenty or twenty-two. But he was shrewd . . . he was a shrewd boy . . . the money was new, sequenced, so he laundered it over time . . . buying a packet of cigarettes with large denomination notes for example. The change is clean money, can't be traced when you put it in your bank account."

"Clever boy."

"Patient as well. He told me it took him three years to launder it. It was then that he moved to York, bought property and began life as a crook, and eventually settled on blackmail. One good sting every year or two, he said, that's all it takes. Told me his wife and son never knew about it, said he told them he was just a Mr Ten Per Cent with a few legitimate interests as a smokescreen. Then he said he'd done better than me. 'Did better than you, didn't I? Same school same start, but I did better.'"

"Up to a point," Hennessey said. "I mean, you're still alive, aren't you?"

"The wages of sin, eh?"

"If you like. But let's talk about your sin."

"My sin, deception . . . and poverty. That's a sin . . . allowing yourself to be in poverty."

"You're in poverty?"

"The house may look impressive, but I've hardly eaten into the mortgage. At my age I should have more equity than I have. Ossler saw to that. The house in France is really only a converted pigeon loft, but it's cheaper than going to the Mediterranean for a fortnight and it's not really saleable, the market for holiday homes being what it is. Now my income has dried up. Poverty."

"Do you own a gun?"

Silence. West glanced at Hennessey. "No," he said.

"Not the most truthful man in the Vale are you?"

A look of anger flashed across West's eyes. "Am I under suspicion?"

"Of course you are, Mr West. In fact you're now in the unenviable position of being prime suspect in the murder of Nathan Ossler."

"I didn't kill Ossler!"

161

"So you say. So anyone would. You see, Mr West, this murder was premeditated so no one's going to come stumbling into the police station in distress, full of confession and regret." Hennessey paused. "It's going to be up to us to find the murderer with sufficient proof that he did it. But you can help yourself or you can hinder yourself. A confession will be in your best interest."

"No." West shook his head. "It'll be in the best interest of the murderer. I didn't kill Ossler." He gripped the table. Rage was in his eyes. "I didn't kill Ossler."

"What did he do? Put the squeeze on for more money? Didn't keep his promise to go away once you'd paid up? Recognised you as a good touch and returned to really clean you out? So you shot him with the handgun you didn't surrender during the amnesty?"

"Fantasy. Pure fantasy."

"Is it? Look at if from our point of view for a second, will you? I have heard from people that if someone spends too long in the teaching profession, they have difficulty opening their minds to the point of view of others. But try, just try. Point one, you have motivation. Even if you had paid up and even if he wasn't putting extra squeeze on you, he was still alive, living in close proximity to you and holding information that could destroy you. It was worth the risk to go to his house and blow his brains out."

"I did not kill Ossler."

"Point two, we now find that you have a familiarity with firearms, you're a member of a gun club, no less."

"Means nothing."

"Means a lot. And you're certainly intelligent enough not to be caught in possession of the gun, so the absence of the gun when we search your house . . ."

"You're going to search my house?"

"Have to. Grounds here for a warrant to do said thing. Why, what are we going to find that you don't want us to find?"

"Nothing."

"But we won't find the gun because you dismantled it and dropped it in the Ouse, or in a stream or in a water trough in the middle of a field, the sort that cows drink from and the sort the farmers never let run dry." Hennessey paused. "And you have no alibi. No alibi at all. Walking round York because it was a pleasant evening . . . a headmaster who has to be up bright and early to take morning assembly. Come on. And you keep a dog. So you know dogs, so you'll know how to get past Ossler's Alsatians. And you've also got the personality for it, Mr West. I've been a police officer a long time, close to retiring now, and I've seen that look in your eyes, the eyes of other killers . . . there is a murderer personality and you've got it, a low flash point, an outrageous sense of your own importance. You can't get a university degree, so you'll invent one. That's ego mania. You're a 'control freak', so called, dominate the world around you, dominate the school, dominate your wife and children, and along comes Ossler and has you dancing on the end of his string like a puppet. That would not go down too well with a control freak, that alone would be enough to make you want to murder him, a control freak who's being controlled."

Hennessey leaned forward. "Nigel West, I am arresting you in connection with the murder of Nathan Ossler. You do not have to say anything but it may harm your defence if you do not mention when questioned something you later rely on in court. Anything you do say may be given in evidence."

Mr Crowther turned to West and said, "Say nothing."

Hennessey paused, then said. "This interview is concluded at twelve fifteen p.m."

163

Seven

In which George Hennessey benefits from a start-
ling revelation and the much misnamed Thundercliffe
Grange is revisited.

T he body had been hidden. That was plain. It was very,
very plain to Melita Burroughs when she found the
body and tugged her spaniel away from it and it was plain
to the white-shirted constables who attended the scene in
response to Melita Burroughs' three nines call, and who then
wound a blue and white police tape from one tree to the next
to the next to the next until it had described a rough square
around a natural hollow in the ground. It was also plain
to George Hennessey who arrived in response to the call
from the attending constables requesting CID attendance.
It was also plain to Melita Burroughs, the two constables
and to Chief Inspector Hennessey that whilst the body had
been hidden, it had not been hidden very thoroughly. It was
hidden as though by someone who didn't intend to remain
in the vicinity but wanted only time to depart, so thought
George Hennessey as he stood in the shade of the copse,
brushing away the flies with his straw hat. A natural hollow,
a corpse, male, going by the parts that protruded from the
mound of rubble which covered it. Hennessey walked from

the copse into the searing heat and the sunlight and blue sky, down the path between wide wheat fields to where Melita Burroughs waited by the police car on which the blue light revolved, as if lapping the parched countryside.

"You found the body, I understand, madam?" Hennessey mopped the perspiration from his brow with his handkerchief. He spoke softly, seeing at first only a frail-looking, elderly lady holding a panting spaniel in a sitting position at the end of a yellow nylon leash. He glanced behind him at the island of green foliage in a sea of wheat that was the copse.

"Aye," she said simply. "Stones had been disturbed, local lads, I reckon. Saw the skull and panicked. I came along, saw the same thing but didn't panic. Walked home to the village, phoned the police, walked back. Met them here, told them what to find and where to find it."

"Doesn't seem to upset you, Mrs . . . ?"

"Miss. No, it doesn't bother me. I'm a retired nurse. I've seen it all, living and dead. And I'm a Christian, people die. It is the way of it."

Hennessey mopped his brow again. This time it was he who said, "Aye". Frail and elderly, Miss Burroughs might be but he saw that she was clearly in full possession of her faculties and that her psyche was made of steel. He pulled the brim of his panama down against the glare of the sun.

"I live in the village. Tess and I walked to the wood each day. It's a bit warm for her body but not too warm. She'll cope. I can, so she can."

Hennessey glanced at the springer spaniel, tongue well out, panting, but the eyes were alert. He didn't think the animal seemed too distressed. "I've got a dark-coloured dog too," he told her. "In this weather, we walk in the evenings, it's more comfortable for him."

Melita Burroughs snorted her disdain at Hennessey's attitude to his dog. Hennessey found a moment to ponder that nurses are like teachers: always right about everything, all the time.

"So, you found the body?" He pressed forward.

"Sara found it. Some of the rubble which wasn't there yesterday had become dislodged."

"The rubble wasn't there yesterday?"

"No. Anyway, I saw the skull, returned home, phoned the police. Told them an incinerated corpse had been partially hidden, that was to frustrate identification, I should think. Then the rubble was placed on top of it."

"You think?"

"Fairly obvious I'd say. And it was burnt there. Not burnt elsewhere and carried there."

"Again, you think?"

"Again fairly obviously, there is burning to the leaves and branches of the shrubs near the hollow. The flames have clearly scorched the vegetation."

"I'd go along with that." Hennessey looked up as a red and white Riley circa 1947 approached the scene, being driven slowly, sedately even, one of the more comforting aspects of the branch of medicine known as forensic pathology, so observed Hennessey. Not for Louise D'Acre and others of her ilk the pressure of life-saving minutes of accident and emergency work.

"Would have been done yesterday between noon and about five p.m." Melita Burroughs said sharply, bringing Hennessey's mind back to focus on the matter in hand. "I was in the wood yesterday, late morning, the children play

166

there after school hours from five p.m. onwards, during term time, and all day out of term time and at weekends. It's term time at the moment, so he was burnt there yesterday afternoon, set alight and covered with rubble. There's plenty of rubble about, there used to be an old barn nearby, I well remember it from my girlhood. It was demolished some years ago but the site was never properly cleared. I've helped you all I can." She stood. "You won't need to detain me any longer. The constable has my address. Come on, Tess."

Hennessey, both amused and flabbergasted, watched her go. He was disinclined to argue and was happy to let her go on her terms sensing that Melita Burroughs would probably be more difficult than the most delinquent youth. Further, and if, he thought, if he was to be at all honest, he relished more the prospect of the company of Louise D'Acre than he relished the continued presence of Melita Burroughs and he watched proudly as the former stepped out of the Riley, rotating her bottom, keeping both slender legs together as she opened the forward hinging door of the classic motor car. She stood and closed the door behind her, built like a willow wand, short haired, serious minded. She walked towards Hennessey. "Good day, Inspector."

"Dr D'Acre," Hennessey responded formerly. "One charred male corpse for your consideration."

"Very well, lead on please."

Hennessey led on and he and the forensic pathologist walked from the lane along the path between golden fields to the shade of the copse and to the charred corpse in a hollow in the ground.

"Well." Dr D'Acre snapped on a pair of latex gloves. "You know, Inspector, I find it passing ironic that . . . well . . . lighten our darkness and preserve us from all

167

perils and dangers of this night . . . what are perils and dangers for some are meat and drink to the likes of me . . . what peril and danger befell yon, I wonder?"

"I have every confidence you'll be able to tell us, Dr D'Acre. I'll get a constable to remove the rubble."

"Or even volunteer to do it yourself, Chief Inspector?" She smiled, holding eye contact. "Or even myself." She bent down and began to toss the lumps of rubble aside with seemingly minimal effort and Hennessey saw again how her slender build belied a muscular body and that far from complaining, even in good humour, that he had to compete for attention with her horse, it was her horse riding that had developed a body tone which had given so much to their sex life. He bent down and helped her remove the rubble. She glanced at him, their eyes met, his so warm and brown, as if to say ". . . love you". But then she froze him with a stare which said "remember what we agreed, work is work". Then she returned her attention to the removal of the rubble from the charred corpse.

The body, fully exposed, revealed itself to be a heavily built, young-looking male. The corpse had been partially incinerated about the head, destroying the facial features, the lower body, the legs and arms had not been burned. All clothing remained intact.

"Male, mid to late twenties." Louise D'Acre held a small battery-operated tape recorder close to her mouth and spoke in her soft, learned manner. "Significant thermal injuries to face and head . . . the teeth also seem to have been subject to trauma, possible in a further attempt to frustrate identification by matching with dental records. The corpse appears to be possibly about twenty-four hours *post mortem*, and has been burnt at the scene . . . there is

thermal damage to vegetation beside and above the corpse."
She paused.

"Point to Miss Burroughs." Hennessey brushed at the
swarm of flies above the corpse with his arm but made
little impression on the determination of the insects.

"Sorry?"

"Nothing. Just that the lady who discovered the body
made the same observation . . . about the burning to the
foliage, I mean." He pondered her marching briskly back
to the village, her and Tess, sun or no sun.

"Oh . . ." Louise D'Acre viewed the corpse. "There's
a significant tattoo on the left forearm, obviously a self-
inflicted tattoo of the sort that children give themselves in
children's homes and this one clearly reads 'Ark Royal',
that may help with the identification, Mr Hennessey." She
replaced the tape recorder in her bag and took out a small
electronic camera and photographed the tattoo. The sudden
flash dazzled Hennessey. She took another, wider angled
photograph of the corpse and then replaced the camera in
her bag. "If you could help me turn him over, I'll be able
to take a rectal temperature and then a ground temperature,
it'll help me determine the time of death. Then we can get
him to the laboratory." She too then waved her arm about
the swarm of flies. "Have to hurry, won't be much left of
him if we don't."

"Of course." Hennessey took hold of the shoulders. "But
I know him."

"You do?" Louise D'Acre took the feet of the corpse.
"Clockwise, one, two, three . . ."

"Yes." Hennessey laid the corpse gently, face down. "I've
seen him recently. I think I know who he is . . . the age . . .
the build . . . the inexpensive clothing. You know there's a

poignancy about realising that you are looking at a corpse which just a few hours earlier you saw as a living, breathing person, in this case, with his life ahead of him. Reminds you of your own mortality."

"Certainly does, Mr Hennessey." Louise D'Acre stood. "Well, if you could get a couple of constables to put him in a body bag? As young and inexperienced as possible?"

Hennessey glanced at her, questioningly.

"Well," she said, "what I mean is, if they haven't handled a dead body before, it's as well to do it for the first time in a lovely setting like this, on a lovely day like this, under the supervision of experienced people like thee and me. Don't you think?"

Three hours later, in the pathology laboratory of York District Hospital, Louise D'Acre switched off the overhead microphone and covered the corpse with a sheet and stepped back, allowing the mortuary attendants to lift the body on to a trolley and wheel it to the storage area. She approached Hennessey who had been observing the post-mortem for the City of York Police. "Did you get the gist of that?" she asked, as she peeled off the gloves.

"He was shot," said Hennessey. "Confess that rings bells."

"Does, doesn't it? Second this week, and in the Vale of York. Getting more like Dodge City every day. The bullet was small calibre .22 I think. Nasty little guns I'm told. Penetrate a long way into the body. A long way into the brain in this case, into the back of the head and all the way to the front, but didn't exit. He wasn't shot at close range. The bullet's in one piece . . . I'll clean it up and send it to the forensic science laboratory . . . the gunshot killed him, the thermal injury is *post mortem*, no soot in the trachea. If he had been breathing when alight, there'd be soot deposits in his throat. But there are none."

"So he was iced, then fired?"

"Is not a very scientific but very succinct way of putting it."

"So long as I grasp the nuts and bolts."

"Simply no indication of prior injuries, or of his body being dragged to where it was found, so he walked knowing or unknowing to his death."

"Lured there or marched there at gunpoint, you mean?"

"Yes," Louise D'Acre nodded. "That's exactly what I mean. His teeth had been smashed, again, *post mortem*, little bleeding you see, possibly as an after thought, after the fire had done its damage."

"Time of death, you think?"

"Yesterday, possibly yesterday afternoon."

"That ties in with other evidence," Hennessey said. "The lady who found him walks in the wood each day with her dog and she was certain the corpse wasn't there yesterday lunchtime and she believes it may have been found by children playing in the wood that evening who were too scared to report what they had found."

"I can understand that. Tough on them, though," Louise D'Acre grimaced. "The bullet seems to have travelled upwards as it passed through the brain, suggesting that the person who pulled the trigger was shorter than the deceased."

"Shorter?" Hennessey echoed, as his thoughts began to turn towards a slightly built, almost anorexic young woman of his recent acquaintance.

"The deceased was in his mid to late twenties. I'll divide

a tooth in cross section, that'll provide his age to within twelve months. A beer drinker, his stomach was bloated by the ingestion of much carbohydrate, apart from that, the only thing in his stomach was a bit of bacon and bread."

"Bacon sandwich?"

"Would be my guess. My favourite snack in fact. Lovely. Not particularly healthy, but it goes well with the lifestyle of a man who consumes much beer. And that, Chief Inspector, will be my findings, and to be reported to you in much more scientific language, but that, as you say, is the nuts and bolts of it. I took a clearer photograph of the tattoo, as you saw. I'll get a copy to you a.s.a.p."

"Thanks. That'll be one for the press release, BBC and ITV regional news and the *Yorkshire Post* tomorrow. Mind you, I think I know who the victim is and the .22 bullet pretty well clinches it, but I'd prefer someone to feed me a name. If no one does, I'll proceed on what our American cousins would call a 'hunch', but I prefer to do things a little more methodically, if I can."

Jeremy Aitken missed the evening news. He was working the late shift. The following morning, the Thursday of that week, he left his modest three-bedroom house in Huntingdon and walked the short distance to the newsagent's and bought a copy of that day's edition of the *Yorkshire Post*. On the front page was the photograph of the tattoo observed on the arm of the partly incinerated corpse which had been found the previous day by Miss Burroughs. The "full story" was, it read, on page three. Jeremy Aitken said, involuntarily "oh . . . no . . ." and turned to the story before he had purchased the newspaper.

"Trouble?" The stockily built, gruff spoken newsagent looked genuinely concerned. His shop smelled of sweets.

"Not for me." Aitken fumbled in his pocket for loose change. "I know this lad. I recognise the tattoo."

"He was murdered."

"So I see." He handed the newsagent the correct money for the newspaper.

"Shot in the head."

"Poor lad. I'd better give the police a phone call."

"You can do it from here."

"No . . . I'll do it from home." Which he did immediately upon his return. George Hennessey knocked politely on his door three-quarters of an hour later.

Hennessey found Aitken to be a gentle-mannered man, slight, balding, bespectacled, modest in manner and, thought Hennessey, utterly unsuitable to be working with demanding, delinquent adolescents, which, he was informed, was the nature of his occupation. Hennessey knew that such adolescents were children only in terms of their age, in name only, and he more than suspected that they knowingly exploit their protected status in the eyes of the law, to perpetrate murderous assaults and highly organised robberies. A gentle man like Aitken, Hennessey mused, could not have an easy working life.

"It was the tattoo," said Aitken as he and Hennessey sat down opposite each other on inexpensive furniture in a room decorated with children's paintings.

"I hoped that it would jog someone's memory. So it was Shane Widestreet. That's the second time this week a tattoo has provided an identification."

"Really?" Aitken smiled warmly.

"Yes, really, and there's a possible connection too. We

173

can possibly confirm his ID by matching dental records. Some of his teeth were damaged, but not all, there may be sufficient to provide a match."

"Well the tattoo was unique, 'Ark Royal'. He tattooed himself, as disturbed children do. A pin pushed through an ink-saturated ball of cotton wool. The ink stains the skin where it's punctured, it's pretty effective, crude, untidy, but effective. You can always tell adults who've been in care as children, they'll often have such tattoos on their arms or on the back of their hands. It's an expression of self-loathing, so we are told, during our all too infrequent in-service training. But Shane wanted to join the Royal Navy, hence the tattoo. He even put himself up for admission but failed the medical and was quite upset about it for a long time, one more rejection you see. He was a sensitive lad, he hurt easily and felt deeply. He developed an overbearing macho man image and wore male jewellery for a while, but it was just to hide the timid little boy inside."

"I'm surprised his sister hasn't come forward to identify him. We know she's in York."

Aitken frowned. "He doesn't have a sister."

Hennessey felt his mouth open slightly. "No sister?"

"No. No, Shane was alone in the world. He was abandoned by his mother when he was young, never knew his father. A succession of social workers tried to place him with foster parents but for one reason or another he was deemed 'hard to place' and effectively grew up in care. If he had had a sister, we would have known about it. He left us for a supported tenancy in Tang Hall."

"He's still there. Or at least he was until about lunchtime yesterday. A woman called Sadie . . . does that ring any bells? They claimed to be brother and sister."

174

"Sadie . . ." Aitken repeated. "Slightly built, dark-haired girl?"

"Yes."

"Oh, poor Shane . . . that must have been Sadie Kuppe."

"Kuppe?"

"K. u. p. p. e.," Aitken said. "She insisted it was pronounced Kuppa, as in a 'cuppa' tea. I knew they picked up with each other, didn't think they continued it when they were discharged, but we heard that they got married."

"Oh." Hennessey sat back and heard the inexpensive chair creak against his weight. "So they were husband and wife . . . not brother and sister at all. Well, well . . . that answers a few questions such as the sleeping arrangements in Shane's tiny, one-room tenancy. Tell me about Sadie Kuppe?"

"Quite a different kettle of fish to Shane. She and he were opposites on pretty well every level. Shane was soft hearted and easily led, a bit touchy about his surname but really soft as putty, Sadie was cold and calculating and manipulative. Shane had feelings, Sadie was utterly detached. We knew where Shane came from, Sadie was of travelling stock, some travellers were moving south for the winter, they were passing through York and a group of them tried to steal a car, they were disturbed and bolted, but Sadie tripped and turned her ankle, so she was collared. She would only give her name and age as fourteen, as it was then, and none of the travellers would claim her as their own and they left York a day or two later. We had no one to discharge her to and so we had to keep her. Can't fathom that sort of thinking, your kith and kin . . ." Aitken shook his head.

"They probably thought she'd abscond and join up with them in due course."

"Probably, but she seemed to take to the children's home, quite different from a traveller's life. But a hard girl, fought like a demon, the other children always gave her a wide berth, so I was worried for Shane when Sadie got her talons into him. She also gave the impression that something dreadful had happened to her . . . gave her a mean streak . . . maybe that's why she wasn't so keen to catch up with her family."

"Maybe."

"Sadie was quite dishonest, underhand as well. Some children were honest about their bad behaviour. I mean, for example, picking fights with the staff, being seen to vandalise things, there's something honest about that, but when Sadie came there began a series of incidents which could only be described as sabotage . . . damage done to things but the authorship of the damage was never identified. After a while we came to believe it was all down to Sadie Kuppe."

"I am beginning to get the picture of her."

"Are you? She'd never argue with a member of staff, but would put broken glass beneath the tyres of a car belonging to a member of staff who might have picked her up for something. In war she'd be a sniper, quite a good one too. That's how I recall her, but what she's like now, I can't tell you. People change, I wouldn't be in this line of work if I didn't believe that people can change. If people can't change there's just no hope for the world."

"None at all," Hennessey smiled in agreement. "Though I'm less convinced that people do change very much than I was when I was younger. And some folk don't change at all. Of that I am certain."

"Police work has made you cynical, Mr Hennessey."

"It goes with the territory, Mr Aitken."

"Her coping mechanisms were desperate," Aitken continued. "If you had some evidence of her wrongdoing, she'd still swear blind that it wasn't her, or else she'd just turn away and stare at the corner of the room or out of the window, knowing that eventually you'd go away, ostrich-like, except that ostriches don't do that, they don't stick their heads into holes in the ground if danger threatens."

"Don't they?"

"No. That's a myth. Ostriches take flight, by which I mean they run if danger threatens, and they can put on quite a turn of speed. If you think about it, every species has to have a valid survival mechanism. If ostriches really did stick their heads into holes to escape from danger, assuming such holes were always so conveniently placed, the species probably wouldn't survive predation."

"It wouldn't, would it?" Hennessey grinned.

"But that 'ostrich mentality' was Sadie Kuppe's coping mechanism. Staff would say, 'Come on Sadie, why did you do it, the answer's not out of the window . . . why did you do it?' But she'd just stand there, knowing that eventually the member of staff would give up and go away. She knew that if she stood there long enough, just staring out of the window she'd get away with it, whatever 'it' happened to be. But mostly, she did get away with it because whenever we found the damage, there was nothing to link it to Sadie."

"But you knew it was she?"

"Oh, yes. We got to know her paw print, never a lot of force, nothing prolonged, but whatever she did would be very efficient. A good return on the investment. If Shane was shot in the head like the *Yorkshire Post* reports, then

177

that is classic Sadie, a bullet in the head, minimal effort, massive damage. You know, I shouldn't be saying this, but if Sadie did murder Shane, I'd rather like to be a fly on the wall when you interview her. She can stare at the corner of the room or out of the window all she likes, the police won't go away."

Hennessey returned to Micklegate Bar Police Station and asked the collator to access the Police National Computer for information, if any, on one Kuppe, Sadie, aged twenties. "Won't be many Kuppes," he added. He replaced the phone and made a mug of coffee and stood by the window drinking it while looking out on the sun-baked street and the tourists and townsfolk alike in brightly coloured, summer clothing. A person glancing at him from the street might have thought him a man blessed with an easy life, but in fact George Hennessey was deep in thought. His thoughts were interrupted by the collator knocking on his door and breezing cheerfully into his office.

"This is what you want, sir," he said, smiling and holding a computer printout in his hand.

"Thanks." Hennessey took the printout and returned to his desk as the collator left the room.

Sadie Kuppe had, it seemed, been committing offences since the age of sixteen when she was convicted of shop-lifting, actually on her sixteenth birthday. The kindly magistrates bound her over in the sum of ten pounds, and doubtless, Hennessey thought, she had left the court smirking from ear to ear, given the picture Jeremy Aitken had painted of her. He was reminded of the observation made by criminologists that a severe, even custodial sentence for a first offence seems to prevent re-offending, whereas lenient sentencing seems to lead on to further and eventual habitual offending. Maybe if the beaks of the York bench had been less soft-hearted when slight and slender Sadie Kuppe, in care of the social services and living in a children's home, had been brought before them . . . perhaps . . . perhaps . . . He continued to read and found that a pattern of non-violent offences emerged, fraud in the main, though she had avoided custodial sentences. Hennessey found himself pondering the irony of Ossler blackmailing Hargrave or Humby for bigamy, when all the while . . . how rich, how rich. He read on and noted that she had once been the interest of the Greater Manchester Police, the interested constable being one Detective Sergeant Keith Stebbings of the Central Division. Hennessey phoned the Central Division on the off-chance that DS Stebbings might be available. He was.

"Oh, her . . ." Stebbings spoke with a strong Lancashire accent. "Has she surfaced again? Rather fancy she would. So, she's gone back to using her maiden name."

"You knew her by another name?"

"Cloch," said Stebbings. "*The* Cloch, sportswear manu-facturers. You might have seen the name on T-shirts and training shoes that joggers wear. There's a very attractive girl in our street and the name bounces past our house at about seven each evening."

"That Cloch!" Hennessey grinned, allowing his smile to be heard down the phone.

"That Cloch. Ivan Cloch by name. Though the business has folded now, she sold up after he was murdered."

Hennessey groaned, he knew what was coming, but he asked to hear the story anyway.

"Poor Ivan, devoted his life to building up his company, realised he had made it at the expense of remaining single

179

and childless, so he advertised for a wife of childbearing age . . . didn't make any bones about it. Essentially he was looking for breeding stock. He wanted someone to carry the business on after him. Sadie Kuppe answered the ad. She told us that most of the respondents were at the very end of their childbearing years, so Ivan had told her, but she was twentysomething and not unattractive. There was no contest. They married quickly at a Manchester registry office."

"And he was murdered shortly afterwards and she had a cast-iron alibi, possibly involving her brother?"

A pause.

"Yes . . ." Stebbings said cautiously. "Why? Does it sound familiar?"

"Yes, in fact," Hennessey replied softly. "Mrs Cloch, née Kuppe is now Ossler, a widowed lady whose wealthy and much older husband was shot late last Sunday evening, when Mrs Ossler was visiting Shane Widestreet, who is in fact her first husband. At least he was until he was found shot, partially incinerated and buried under a pile of rubble in a wood just outside York. That was this morning."

"Well . . . we just assumed they were brother and sister . . . come to think of it, they didn't look like siblings, he so big and biddable, her so small and feisty. We just didn't check. I feel a bit awkward."

"We had a break you didn't have." Hennessey moved the phone from one ear to the other. Shane Widestreet had a distinct tattoo, we used it as part of an appeal for information and we were contacted by a gentleman who knew both Shane and Sadie when they were in care. After that it all fell into place, for us anyway, for little Miss Kuppe it all fell apart.

"She's in custody?"

"Not yet. Saw you were involved. Thought I'd phone you. Pleased I did."

"I'm pleased you did. I'd like to come and see her. We have a few questions for her as well."

"I'm sure that can be arranged in the next day or two."

"Greed."

"I'm sorry?"

"Greed. That was her motivation. She pulled it off once, made herself a wealthy woman. Ivan Cloch left her everything, house, thriving business, assets, we were looking for culprits in the Manchester business community. She was visiting her brother in York at the time, her alibi seemed to check out, she was never in the frame."

"How was her husband killed?"

"Shot. A well-placed bullet in the back of his head."

"Small calibre?"

"Yes, .22 I recall. A real killer's gun if you know where to put the bullet. So she went back to York and kept up the poor girl image, couldn't flaunt that wealth without inviting suspicion, but she'll have close on a million quid tucked away somewhere. Then did one more by the sound of it, one more to make sure, then head for the sun."

"But not before she got rid of husband number one, whose usefulness had expired."

"All falls into place, as you say. Oh . . . you still there . . . ?"

"Yes?"

"The bullet. I remember now. It exploded on impact. Dumdum I think they're called."

Richard Hargrave or Humby, was released from custody having been charged with attempting to pervert the course

181

of justice by laying false information before the registrar of births, marriages and deaths, but he didn't seem to be listening as he was being charged, he seemed away in a different world, or frightened of the world which waited for him outside the safety of the police station. Nigel West was charged with one specimen charge of obtaining money by dishonesty, namely his most recent salary cheque and was asked to return to the police station the following Monday "to be interviewed". He too, seemed to be thinking himself elsewhere as he was discharged from custody, but then glanced at the bemused custody sergeant and said, "You know the irony is that I was good at it . . . I really was good at the job. It may have been dishonest, but I really did earn it."

"Yes, sir," the custody sergeant said. "Just sign for your belongings, just here, on the line. Thank you."

Hennessey and Yellich and two constables, one male, one female, convoyed in two cars to Shane Widestreet's address in Tang Hall. There was no answer to the loud, confident, but not aggressive knocking on the door. Yellich walked to the rear of the tenancy and came back and shook his head. "Nothing, sir," he said.

"She left this morning. Her and the dogs. Drove away in a car, a taxi." The officers turned. The owner of the voice was a neighbour, who stood in the knee-high grass of her front lawn. She had a round, ruddy face and, thought the officers, could have been anywhere from thirty to fifty years of age. This is Tang Hall, where life can be hard.

"She left?" Hennessey echoed.

"This morning. Not going far though. Only carried a small bag."

"Thanks." Hennessey turned to Yellich and the male constable. "Put the door in, please."

Hennessey didn't know what he expected to find in the small, cramped tenancy, and he didn't find it. The flat was very Tang Hall, cluttered, clothes strewn, unwashed dishes in the sink, refuse spilling out of black bin-liners which rested against the grease-caked sink unit and there were flies, many flies, buzzing in the shade, enjoying feasting. But the officers found nothing, nothing at all to attract the attention of the police: no documents about offshore accounts, no firearms, just a small, unclean and untidy council house.

Yellich glanced at Hennessey. "There's only one place she can be, boss."

Hennessey nodded. "I think you're right, Yellich. I think you're right."

Sadie Ossler was located at Thundercliffe Grange. She opened the door to Hennessey and Yellich and the two constables, held eye contact with them and then retreated into the building. Hennessey and Yellich and the constables followed her, through the kitchen, past two growling Alsatians, and into the living-room of the house. Clothing and a half-packed suitcase rested on the settee. A generously proportioned leather shoulder bag sat on the coffee table.

"Going somewhere, Sadie?" Hennessey asked.

Sadie Ossler or Widestreet or Cloch, née Kuppe, stared out of the window but didn't reply.

Hennessey stepped forward and picked up the shoulder bag and delved inside. He extracted a brown envelope, took the paper it contained and read the contents. "You're a wealthy woman, Sadie." He passed the document to Yellich. "Offshore accounts in the Cayman Islands, no less."

Sadie Ossler stood and stared blankly out of the window.

183

"Three husbands, Sadie, all shot. Two very rich and one very useful, there to alibi you because you told him to do so. Isn't that right?" Hennessey paused. "Come on, Sadie, the answer's not out of the window. You're not in the children's home now, the Majesty of the law won't get tired and go away."

No reply. Just a continued steady stare at the front lawn.

"Calling it a won game were you, Sadie? Leaving a forwarding address with a solicitor, so he could send you what you were going to inherit from Mr Ossler's estate after he'd wrapped it up and sold it. Was that your plan?" He delved further into the bag. "What were you and your husband, who you said was your brother, drinking that night in the pub, alcohol-free lager to keep your heads clear? A drive out to Strensall in a hire car parked some distance from the house? No problem getting past the dogs for you, was there, Sadie? Found your husband in his study . . . he stood up because he was surprised to see you, and even more surprised to see a gun in your hand. Then you shot him, once in the head, with a bullet that would fragment on impact . . ." Hennessey paused, Yellich saw him frown and then watched as he pulled a small calibre gun from the shoulder bag. The two officers glanced at each other. "Sadie . . . the bullet in Shane's head that didn't explode . . . did you know that? If it proves to have been fired from this gun then you really have got some explaining to do . . . Sadie? Mrs Ossler? Do you hear what I'm saying . . . I'm going to arrest you for the murder of three men."

The female constable took her handcuffs from her waist pouch and advanced on Sadie Ossler.

Sadie Ossler continued to look at the lawn, and then began to smile a very vacant smile.

Turnbull, Peter, 1950-
Perils and dangers

	DATE DUE		
	DISCARDED FROM THE		
	PORTVILLE FREE LIBRARY		
	2-3-20		